EcoErotica

By Selena Kitt

eXcessica publishing

EcoErotica © 2008 by Selena Kitt

All rights reserved under the International and Pan-American Copyright Conventions. No part of this book may be reproduced or transmitted in any form or by any means, electronic or mechanical, including photocopying, recording, or by any information storage and retrieval system, without permission in writing from the publisher.

This is a work of fiction. Names, places, characters and incidents are either the product of the author's imagination or are used fictitiously, and any resemblance to any actual persons, living or dead, organizations, events or locales is entirely coincidental. All sexually active characters in this work are 18 years of age or older.

This book is for sale to ADULT AUDIENCES ONLY. It contains substantial sexually explicit scenes and graphic language which may be considered offensive by some readers. Please store your files where they cannot be access by minors.

Excessica LLC
486 S. Ripley #164
Alpena MI 49707

To order additional copies of this book, contact:
books@excessica.com
www.excessica.com

Cover art © 2016 Willsin Rowe
First Edition November 2010

Warning: the unauthorized reproduction or distribution of this copyrighted work is illegal. Criminal copyright infringement, including infringement without monetary gain, is investigated by the FBI and is punishable by up to 5 years in prison and a fine of $250,000.

Introduction

I have to laugh every time I see the line, "Where are we going? And why are we in this handbasket?" But it isn't really funny.

When I was a kid, I remember having a progressive teacher who talked about something called "Earth Day." It was a pretty new thing, the idea that we might harm the planet we lived on in some way. Earth Day back then was all about recycling tin cans and turning out the lights when you left the room, But no one talked about the important things—like our dependence on fossil fuels.

As I'm writing this, the cost of gas has moved past four dollars a gallon, and experts say it isn't likely to see the underside of three dollars a gallon again. It's already having deep economic consequences as Americans—who stereotypically drive home forty miles from work to our huge McMansions in our SUVs to dine on food grown, for the most part, in some foreign country—are starting to realize on a more global level how much we, personally, are going to be touched by our lack of foresight when it comes to the environment.

You see, I have a theory—people don't really start paying attention to something until it touches their lives, until it becomes personal. Until then, most people remain comfortably oblivious. When their own world is touched, however, then they start to notice. This happens individually, over and over, until the idea becomes global and enters the collective consciousness of the culture.

The number of things wrong with our world when it comes to environmental issues would take entirely too long to list, but people have tried. Scientists have issued warnings, journalists have reported, people have blogged, politicians have made speeches, even documentaries, to highlight the dangers we're facing as a population, not just here in the U.S., but all over the globe, on a mass environmental scale.

Finally, people are starting to listen.

This anthology came about because environmental issues are important to me, and I wanted people to feel what it might be like to be personally touched by some sort of environmental problem. Some of the stories here take these issues head on, and some are more subtle, but all of them have one primary goal in mind—to make you care enough about the characters to get you to care about the issues. To that end, I hope it's successful, and that the people who walk and talk on these pages move you, touch you, and give you a reason to care.

Oh, and I definitely hope these sexy, environmentally provocative stories rock your world—and arouse and raise more than just your environmental awareness!

Table of Contents

Cry Wolf	1
Law of Conservation	23
Lightning Doesn't Strike Twice	49
The Break	57
Paved Paradise	77
Genesis	91
Bonus: Core Deep	123

Cry Wolf

Anana watched Davis playing with his toy. He was like a boy, his eyes bright, fiddling with dials and pushing buttons. He was staring at the lime green horizon on the North Slope of Alaska, trying to make a connection between his electronic satellite data and the thickening yellow clouds rolling in.

The clouds told her something. A storm was coming.

She gathered the stuff of her camp, her cooking pot, her *ulu*—a half-moon shaped knife that women used for everything from skinning animal hides to chopping ice—and took them into her makeshift sod house.

She could have packed a tent, like Davis, but even though she had been to college in Juneau, and had been tracking with the Wildlife Conservation for nearly five years, there were things she held onto, continuing to follow many of the old ways—each brick in her sod house had been carved out of the earth with her *ulu*.

They had been here observing the pack for a month now. The pups were almost old enough for Davis to fit with collars, or so he kept saying. If he didn't hurry, winter would be upon them, and the wolves would be gone, traveling long distances at night on terrain that they could not follow.

She heard him walking around outside. They could both walk upright when the older wolves were gone and the pups were tucked into the den with their wolf-babysitter. Anana had named him *Maguyuk,* for he was always howling, groveling, whining and rolling onto his back to show the white of his belly. He was the lowest wolf in the caste.

"Anana?" Davis was on his knees, peeking his head into the low entrance of her sod house. "The pack's returning. I think snow's coming."

"Did your fancy toy tell you that?" She smiled, pulling off her fur mittens and laying them on her sod table so she could push her long, thick hair out of her eyes. There was only enough room for her to kneel, and she doubted Davis could do even that.

"When are you going to move into the new millennium, woman?" He winked. "What, are you afraid technology is gonna put you out of business?"

Anana snorted. "If I remember correctly, it wasn't your GPS system that found the wolf den."

She had used a GPS system for a while when she first started, in spite of her father's warning that trackers could become dependent on them. It seemed like an amazing modern convenience, using satellites to pinpoint anything, including your own position. It only took her one night alone on the tundra to realize it was taking too much of her time and energy away from actually tracking—she lost her bearings with it, rather than finding them.

She looked at Davis and saw his smile had wavered into a pout. He grumbled, "Well, you know, I told you—that was just a glitch."

She waved her hand at him. She'd heard it before. "There is an *unalaq*—a strong west wind. It will be a big storm, this one, strange for this time of year. Do you want to stay with me tonight?"

He looked around the small, dark space, frowning. "I think my tent will be fine."

"Let me know if you change your mind." She shrugged. "The pack has returned."

"How—" Davis lifted his head and looked to the west. Anana put her mittens back on, crawling out.

"They will bring meat back for the pups." She edged him out of the way. "I want to see." She crawled up the slope on her belly, her mukluks digging into the frozen ground as she moved her way to the top. Davis trudged his way after her, still carrying his GPS. Anana waved him down and he crouched, beginning to crawl up the slope.

He joined her at the top, the two of them still able to blend into the dark brown and green carpet of the tundra as they peered toward the wolf den. They were well above the tree line here, so there was nothing to mar the vast extent of the landscape, but in the summer, the ground was full of moss and lichens. The pups were out with their babysitter-wolf, Maguyuk, rolling and tumbling and biting on each other's ears. Maguyuk was waiting for the rest of his pack, his nose lifted to the wind.

Anana watched the pups play. The biggest and most playful pup, who she called *Pukiq*, because he was very smart, snuck up behind his sister, *Nukka*, biting her tail.

"They're growing quite big," Anana whispered. Davis nodded, watching in the direction that Maguyuk was looking.

"Wonder how they'll weather this storm?" Davis wondered aloud.

"Wolves have lived out here longer than my ancestors," Anana whispered. "They will survive the weather just fine."

Davis glanced at her and shook his head, smiling.

The three older wolves returned, including the great black wolf leader, his eyes shining as he let Maguyuk mouth his chin, a sign of respect. With that, Maguyuk was off. Anana knew he would backtrack to the kill and eat his fill. The only female wolf was regurgitating food for the pups. Anana had named her *Arnaq*–woman. The pups crowded around to eat, growling happily, their tails wagging.

"Down," Anana hissed, putting her mittened hand on top of Davis' head. Their cheeks rested on the cold ground, facing one another, their breath wafting together in white streams. The temperature was summer still, nearing fall, probably in the high twenties or early thirties, Anana guessed. She knew Davis could have glanced at his watch and told her exactly.

"What is it?" he asked.

"Amaguq." She said the name she had given the leader of the wolf pack and lifted her head very slowly so she could see above the slope. The great black wolf was still watching them, his long snout sniffing the air, although they were downwind.

"The alpha?" Davis lifted his head as well to look. Anana sighed. He called them all by technical names. They were alpha male, alpha female, beta male one and two, all four of them fitted with GPS collars so Davis could track their positions. The pups were also numbered—pups one through six—although up until recently, they had been too young to fit with collars.

"He knows we're here," Anana whispered.

The regal wolf turned twice in a circle and howled, the sound piercing the air. She knew how to live out here, she had done it all of her life, and it had been she who had used her skill to allow them such close access to the wolves' den.

If it had been up to Davis, toting his gun and looking for caribou to hunt, the wolves would have been long gone, she thought. Instead, she made him put his gun away, forced him to rub his tent down in mud to camouflage it, and they had trapped their food and crawled on all fours whenever the wolves were in sight.

She also refused to allow Davis to wear his bright orange parka, making him favor his dark blue one. He had blushed, she remembered, when she joked to him that it brought out the color of his eyes.

"I think he's always known," Davis replied. "Thanks to you, I think he's accepted us."

Anana smiled at his acknowledgement, putting her mittened hand over his.

"This storm may send us home, early," she whispered. "I don't think we're in for any more thaws."

"It doesn't matter," he replied, looking at the GPS in his hand. "Our observation period is over next week. Once I put the interim collars on the pups, we can call the plane to take us back to the mainland."

Was it so soon? she thought. They had been out here for months together, and she had watched the changing of the seasons, the lemmings disappearing, the terns fading in numbers, but her heart didn't seem to want autumn to come.

Anana watched as the third adult wolf, a sleek, silver male she had named *Qopuk,* after the ice, nuzzle Amaguq under the chin. They were a family, although she wasn't quite sure what role this male played in the pack. Best friend, perhaps? He didn't mate with the female, Arnaq—wolves remained monogamous through the season, often through many seasons—but he wasn't the low-man, like Maguyuk, either.

"The storm will be here within the hour," Anana announced, her eyes on the horizon. The arctic terns were circling, and she knew it was over the site of the wolf kill. The clouds were gathering. The sun didn't set, and there was little difference between noon and midnight in the sky now, but storms clouds in the arctic had a strange, lemon yellow tinge, a bright warning against the pale green of evening

"I better pack everything into the tent." Davis turned and slid down the hill on his bottom. Anana rolled over and watched him moving around his camp, gathering equipment. He was a tall man, although all *kablunaks* seemed tall to her. She was just barely five feet, her limbs short, her body compact, with the same broad, flat nose of her ancestors, the same round, moon-like face.

She had grown used to his presence as they tracked the wolves through the beginning summer months. Her primary occupation was tracking, and she'd been taught by her father, and her father's father before him. She grinned as she remembered how angry Davis had been that she was assigned by the conservation department to tag along with him because this was, after all, his first real field assignment. That's how he put it: "I don't want her tagging along." Like she was some annoying little sister.

Walking toward his tent, his part of the camp, she found him squatting on the ground, his parka hood down and his gloves off as he punched information into the GPS in his hand. There was a label along the side of it that read: *Division of Wildlife Conservation Alaska Department of Fish and Game.*

"You are a slave to that thing." She sighed, squatting down beside him. He glanced up at her and smiled.

"I have to admit, I'm beginning to think it's worthless next to you," he replied, slanting her a look.

She raised her eyebrows at him. "Do you want something? What's all this praise about?"

He laughed, turning the GPS off and standing. "You're always questioning my motives."

She watched him stretch and yawn. It was still strange, somehow, to be wide awake at midnight. They were on wolf time now, sleeping during the day and up at night to observe the pack. The passing of time was just the rhythm of life out here on the tundra. He looked down and saw her watching him. She turned her eyes to his tent.

"Are you sure you going to be okay in there?" she asked.

"Listen here," he said with a snort. "That is a North Face VE-25!"

She knew exactly what kind of tent it was, but she didn't tell him so. She just looked at him blankly.

"That tent is pretty much bombproof," he said, looking exasperated. "It's got twelve tie-downs, a geodesic pole design and bar-tacked corner reinforcers."

Anana bit her lip to try to hide a smile. "If you say so."

Davis frowned, looking toward her shelter. "In fact, why don't you stay in with me?"

"In that?" She made a face.

"Yeah, that," he said. "It's gotta be safer than that little hole in the ground you've built. What if you get snowed in?"

She laughed. "So much for praising my abilities." She stood and turned to walk back to her sod house. The wind was already picking up, and it ruffled the wolverine fur trim on her parka.

"I'll see you after the storm," she said. Kneeling down, she crawled into her little hole in the ground.

Anana took off her mukluks and placed them by the door. Then she took off her outer clothing—parka and fur-lined pants—folding them carefully. She continued stripping herself until she was completely nude and everything she had been wearing went into a bag made of a whale bladder, which she was careful to seal tightly against moisture. That was another of the old ways she refused to let go. Her father had told her over and over—damp clothes meant death here in the Arctic.

She shivered in the cold, seeing her own breath as she slid into her sleeping skin. It was a moose hide bag lined in rabbit fur and quite cozy. She pulled it up around her, covering as much of her as she could, so only the top of her head was exposed. She heard the wolves howling. They knew the storm was coming, too. She closed her eyes, and slept.

* * * *

"Anana!" His voice was close, but she couldn't see him at the entrance. Outside, it was a world of white.

"Davis?" She sat up, shivering in the cold, and grabbed her caribou skin off the floor, wrapping it around herself as she made her way to the door. He was wearing full gear, and he was covered in snow as he crawled toward her. She must have slept long, or it must have snowed hard, because the ground was already covered. She could see it built up at the entrance of her house, which she had made the way her father taught her, creating a slanted awning for possibilities such as these.

Anana couldn't see anything past Davis' bulk crawling toward her, not his tent, or the pond, or the slope leading up toward the wolves. It was a white out—the wind a bitter, chilling reminder that this was, indeed, the Arctic.

She reached her hand out and grasped his arm. "How did you find me in this?"

"I don't know." He slid down into her home, landing with a thump on the floor, his breath ragged. "It's gone," he gasped. "Everything is gone. I barely got out of tent before the wind took it."

Anana knelt beside him, taking off his gloves, his hat, unsnapping and unzipping his parka. "We'll find it," she reassured him, putting her fur-warmed hands to his cold, red cheeks.

"There's a foot of snow out there already." His voice was shaking. "I didn't think it would be so much. I didn't put the heavy snow load bearing poles in. With that high west wind, it all piled up on the east side and the tent collapsed."

"You're safe here." Her hands continued to work, undoing his parka.

Davis put his head in his hands and stared at the dirt floor. "You don't understand."

"I understand you're very wet." Anana pushed his parka off his shoulders. "And if you don't get dry, you'll die."

It wasn't as bad as she feared. His Gortex parka and pants were wet, but would dry by morning. His clothes were just a little damp along the edges. Davis let her strip him down to his underwear, which was no easy feat in the small space. It was only then he seemed to notice that she, too, was nude, his eyebrows going up, his eyes raking over her. She laid the caribou skin back on the floor and his clothes on it.

"Now what?" he asked. "All my clothes—everything was in that tent."

"I know." She pulled him along as she crawled toward her sleeping skin. His hand was cold and clammy from the dampness. She'd rubbed him down the best she could. "Here, get in."

He hesitated, looking at her body in the only light coming from the entrance, a hazy, greenish glow. "Anana..."

"Get in," she insisted.

He slid himself into her sleeping skin, and she crawled in beside him, stretching her body against his and pulling the fur up tight around their heads. They lay belly-to-belly, listening to the wind outside.

"The wolves," he whispered.

"Will fare better than your tent." She smiled, but when she saw how devastated he looked, she regretted it. "We'll find it, when the storm is over."

"It could be miles from here by now." Davis sighed. "There aren't any trees to stop it."

"Well, if you don't find it—"

"If we don't find it, we're dead," he told her, his voice flat. "How do you think I was going to send the signal for the plane to take us home? We're stuck out here in the middle of the Arctic tundra with three hundred miles between us and civilization. Just how do you propose we're going to get back? Walk?"

She put her hand over his lips, her eyes soft. "If we have to, yes."

"We have nothing." He shook his head, his eyes dark. "We're as good as dead."

"*Tawia!*" Anana cried and pushed against his chest. "Enough! You are with the best tracker in the Arctic. Do you think I cannot get us home?"

"I—" Davis sighed, closing his eyes. "Let's not talk about it anymore. Okay?"

Anana turned away from him, but there wasn't much room to move, and nowhere to go. Her back was pressed against his belly.

"What kind of fur is this?" Davis asked after a moment, sounding surprised. "It's so warm. I'm always cold, even in my sleeping bag."

"It kept the rabbits warm," she murmured, closing her eyes. The wind was a faint whistle outside the door.

"It's quiet in here," he remarked. She could feel his legs against her feet, less clammy now.

"The earth is a great insulator," she said. "So, do you feel warm now?"

"Yes," he replied. He was quiet again, and then he said, "Thank you."

"You're welcome," she replied, smiling. His chest was rising and falling against her bare back. It was much warmer in her sleeping skin with the two of them.

"I can't sleep," Davis whispered.

She turned her head toward him, smiling. "Do you want me to tell you a story?"

"Tell me how you do it," he said. She felt his hand looking for a comfortable place to rest, settling on her hip. It was warm and large and it made her skin tingle.

"How I do what?"

"Track." Davis curled his body around her. "It's amazing. You see things that I never could."

She felt his breath over her cheek. "That's because you only see what is right in front of you."

"What do you mean?"

"You need to open up the lens of your vision," she said. "Right now, you're looking at my body, yes?"

Davis shifted against her and cleared his throat. "Yes."

"What do you see?"

"Uhhh..."

"The curve of my neck, the slope of my shoulder, maybe?"

She heard the smile in his voice. "Yeah."

"That's tunnel vision," she told him. "Make your eyes go wide angle. Relax your focus. Like you're looking at one of those magic eye puzzles my nephew keeps doing instead of his school work."

"What?"

"Just do it," she urged, pressing her hand to his against her hip. "Now, what do you see?"

Davis propped his head up on his elbow, looking around. "Fur. The earth walls. The caribou skin. That little square clod of packed dirt you call a table."

"Yes." She turned onto her back to look up at him. "Wider. Look at the negative space."

"What?" He shook his head, smiling down at her. She saw his eyes dip below the edge of the sleeping skin, traveling down the length of her body.

"It's not about where I am," she whispered, lifting his chin and directing his eyes back out toward the little room. "It's about where I'm not."

His eyes moved over the room, his face twisted in confusion.

"What are the impressions?" she whispered. "Where have I been?"

"Ohhh," Davis breathed.

"Yes," she smiled up at him, her eyes bright. "It's just like that, tracking wolves, or anything, really. You find the patterns, the subtle shifts, the places where they lived. Everything leaves an impression on the world."

Davis was looking down at her again, his eyes searching. "God, you're beautiful."

"You can touch me."

"I want to."

"I know."

She took his hand and placed it against her breast. They were small and firm, her areolas as dark and round as a new moon. He brushed his thumb over her nipple, which was flat and wide and thick in the middle and very sensitive to touch, watching it harden.

Her face tilted toward his, and he met her mouth. She melted into him, the ache to be with him mounting as his tongue found hers.

She had never been with a *kablunak*, and she was fascinated by his body, how long his limbs were, how light his eyes and hair. She kissed his cheek and the scruffy, dark blonde, three-month beard on his chin, rubbing her cheek there, reveling in the sensation.

"You like that?" He smiled, pulling her hip toward him so they were belly-to-belly again, burying his face in her neck and rubbing his beard over her flesh.

"Davis," she whispered, running her hand over his upper arm, feeling the muscles, tight and hard and sinewy. She tilted her face up again to be kissed and he obliged, his hand moving over the flesh of her back, pulling her in to him. His lips were a soft cloud in the rough landscape of his beard, his mouth a wet cave her tongue dipped in to explore.

They slid easily over the rabbit skin, although there wasn't much wiggle room, their bodies pressed close together. She felt the length of his hardness against her thigh, wanting to impale her like a spear. Outside, the wind howled and the dim light of the storm shed an eerie, beryline light over their faces.

Anana was hungry for him, her little belly rubbing against his, and they worked hard to warm the space with their body heat and ragged breath as they kissed and touched each other. She rolled on top of him, straddling him at the waist, the sleeping skin forcing her to lean forward, her breasts poised near his face. He sucked them, eager, his hips moving them both, up and down, although he wasn't yet inside her.

"Aieeee," she cried as he slipped his hand between her legs, cupping the soft, dark hair of her mound. "Yes, yes." She rocked against him, grinding her pelvis into his hand, urging him with her movements to open her up. He parted her swollen lips, exploring the soft, wet, fleshy folds of her vulva with probing fingers.

She slithered further down his body, reaching between his legs and finding him. He felt enormous in her hand as she tugged and stroked, rubbing him over and over the softness between her legs. Davis held onto her, his fingers digging into the meaty flesh of her hips, moving along with her current, riding the eddies and swirls.

When she sank down onto his shaft, piercing her wet heat with his stiff flesh, Davis groaned, his hands moving around and holding onto the smooth globes of her behind as she began gyrating her hips. Like her ancestors, Anana was soft and curvy, and her shapely, slightly rounded belly rubbed against him as she leaned over and grasped onto his shoulders to steady herself as she rode him.

Her eyes closed as she felt them beginning to meld, their bodies joined in a delicious dance of light and heat and sound. She could hear them crashing together like waves, the wet sound of their flesh merging into one thing. Anana felt as if she were the sea itself, whitecaps cresting and foaming, a constant, pulsing break against the shoreline.

"Ahhhhh!" she cried when his fingers slid up her sides and his hands swallowed her breasts, the mocha color of her skin a sweet, striking contrast to the pale pink of his flesh. Her breath was coming faster, her hair a thick black curtain as she leaned into him.

"Come here," Davis whispered, pulling her to his chest and resting her cheek there. He wrapped his arms around her hips, beginning to thrust up inside of her. She let him do the work now, closing her eyes, the sensation rippling through her, a faster current now. No longer drifting, she was caught in an uprising, a surging tide, heaving her toward some tremendous crash.

"Anana," he whispered, his pelvis rising into hers, his heart beating time against her ear with the rhythm of their bodies. She could feel something shifting inside of her, something immense, tectonic, icebergs moving together in the deep, dark glaciers inching slowly toward liberty.

She moaned, circling him now, her hips moving around and around as he thrust upward, sweeping toward that vast and boundless place that felt as if it might remain just out of her reach for eternity. Beneath her, Davis began driving into her, harder and harder, buoying her upward again and again. She twisted on top of him, burying her face against his shoulder and holding on.

"I can't stop it," Davis whispered, and she felt him let go, a fierce geyser, like the sudden spray of the white whales finally reaching the surface after hours diving below. She felt the winding, rising spiral of her own pleasure mounting to a peak in a gushing swell, sending her soaring like the Arctic terns in a viridian sky.

They lay there merged together, their bodies weak and trembling, listening to the wind moaning outside. Anana stretched herself out, tucking her limbs in and making him her bed. He stroked her hair, kissing her forehead. They both heard the keening wail of a wolf before they drifted off to sleep.

* * * *

She knew the storm was over by the way the light had changed. Davis was still sleeping, his arm thrown over his eyes. He snored. She smiled and stretched against him, finding his mouth and beginning to kiss him awake. She could feel him responding against her thigh. He began to kiss her too, his hands moving to her waist.

"What time is it?" Davis murmured against her cheek.

"You can check your watch," she reminded him. "But I think it must be about noon—so it's really the middle of the night for us."

Davis lifted his wrist to look. "Damn, you're good. Twelve-thirty."

"We should go outside." She rolled off of him and began to wiggle out of the sleeping skin.

"My tent," Davis said, remembering. "My equipment. My data!" He sat up, looking around the small space for his clothing. She brought them to him and they were nearly dry. They dressed in silence, Anana finishing first and poking her head out of the entrance of her the house.

The first snowfall of the year had turned the world into a hushed expanse of land. The birds she had seen and heard calling yesterday were gone, nesting somewhere warm during this strange, early storm.

She knew immediately that Davis' tent was gone. There was nothing left in the spot where it had been, the snow blanketing everything. He crawled out of the entrance, coming to stand beside her.

"Fuck," he said, his voice low, shading his eyes to look further out onto the tundra.

"I'm sorry." She touched his arm. "We can look for it later. Let's check on the wolves."

"They should be sleeping," Davis said.

"So should we," she replied, getting down and beginning to creep up the slope on her belly. It was a different journey in the thick, heavy snow. She guessed it was close to the freezing mark. Davis followed her.

She saw it as soon as she peeked over the top of the slope, and she smiled. The wolves, who Davis said should have been sleeping, were playing, nipping and running and tumbling about twenty feet from where the tent lay mangled and disfigured in the snow.

"My tent!" Davis cried, starting to scramble toward it.

She grabbed his arm, reminding him. "The wolves."

He stopped, looking out at them dancing back and forth together, even the adult wolves heaving and rolling in the white stuff right along with the pups.

"What are they doing awake?" Davis pondered.

"It's the first snow fall of the year," Anana said. "They know it's unusual for it to come so early."

"How am I going to get my tent?" he wondered aloud.

They both knew going out there risked a possible attack, but more likely, it would scare the wolves away from their den. The pups were almost ready to travel, she knew. Amaguq might decide to take them from their summer den early, if a two-legged creature broached their sanctuary.

"I can get it," she told him. "Wait here."

"No," he said, beginning to stand. "It's too dangerous."

She sighed, pulling him back down. "You need to stay down. All fours. Like a wolf."

"You want me to crawl out there?" he asked, his eyes wide.

"That was my plan," she replied with a smile.

Davis snorted. "Some plan. Crawl into the middle of a wolf den?"

Anana watched the wolves. The puppies were climbing all over Arnaq's back. Pukiq had her ear in his mouth, and Nukka had the other. "If you want me to go, I will get your tent."

"No," Davis said again. He sighed. "All fours?"

She nodded, watching Davis start down the slope toward his tent. Amaguq's head raised, his eyes like green sparks.

She hissed, "Slow!" at Davis and then held her breath as she watched him edge closer to his tent. It was a long way to travel on all-fours for someone used to walking on two legs—forty feet, perhaps fifty.

Amaguq barked a warning to his pack and the three adult wolves began herding the pups backwards with their noses, edging them further to the west. The pups wanted to play and clearly hadn't understood Amaguq's concern. He barked toward them again, adding a snarl, and the pups straightened up, allowing their elders to move them along.

Only Amaguq remained, watching Davis crawling along the tundra. The wolf was standing now, hackles raised, growling. She felt an urge to run out there, grab Davis, and pull him back. She fought it. Davis was ten feet from the tent now. He glanced back at her, and then continued to crawl forward, a slow and steady pace.

Amaguq growled as Davis reached his hand out for the tent. She sensed Amaguq was simply protecting his territory. He wasn't planning to attack—to rush forward and spring at Davis—at least she hoped that's what his rounding up of the others to protect the pups meant. Wolves were pack hunters—if he'd meant to hunt Davis, he would have called the other leaders forward, she reasoned.

Davis began dragging his tent with both hands, working his way backward, never turning away from the wolf. Her heart was pounding in her ears. She wished he'd let her go instead. At least then this adrenaline rush could have been focused on something, instead of just sitting in the pit of her stomach like a weight as she watched.

She saw it before she heard it. It was just a faint glimmer in the sky, but it caught her attention. She knew immediately what it was, and what it was looking for. She stood, screaming, "Davis!"

He turned to her, startled, forgetting the tent and the wolf. She pointed to the sky, calling, "Run! Run!" He looked up in the direction she was pointing, seeing the airplane heading toward them. She heard it now, a low buzz. It was a puddle-jumper, a small plane. It was a hunting plane.

"Davis! Run!" she screamed again.

He had his tent in his hands and was pulling it in earnest now, standing and dragging it behind him. Amaguq had heard her scream and he was growling in her direction, his teeth bared. The sound of the plane was closer, and she looked up and saw it flying low. Too low. The tent was a bright orange beacon, making both Davis and the wolf a clear mark.

"Amaguq," she whispered, realizing the immediate danger. She ran down the slope, waving her arms and screaming. "Run! Run! Go away!"

The wolf stood his ground, and she saw the other adult wolves moving forward as she stumbled down the slope in the snow.

"Anana!" Davis grabbed her arm and tugged her back. "What are you doing?"

She faced him, her eyes wild, her mouth twisted. "They're going to kill them!"

"What?" He turned to look at the wolves. Amaguq had been distracted by the two humans in front of him, but now he heard the plane. He barked a warning to the pack and began to run. The plane followed his path.

"No!" She screamed and clutched at Davis as the shot rang out. She saw the black wolf fall to the ground. "Neito, neito, neito!"

"What are they doing up here?" Davis exclaimed. "It isn't hunting season!" He glanced toward the spot where the other wolves had been, but they were disappearing, growing already into faint, moving shadows in the distance.

Anana sobbed as she began running toward the wolf. Davis followed her, panting by her side They saw the plane coming in for a landing. She knelt before the wolf. His blood spread red onto the snow.

"He's dead." She looked up at Davis. His eyes were glazed, as if he were in shock. She sobbed into Amaguq's fur and didn't hear the man approaching until Davis spoke.

"What are you doing up here, Tom?"

Anana's head jerked up at the familiarly and she saw the man coming up to them.

"Hey, Davis." The man knelt into the snow next to the wolf, lifting its head, inspecting it. "They sent us out after the storm to do a little wolf clean-up."

"Wolf... clean-up?" she repeated.

"Who authorized this?" Davis snarled, holding his hand out to her. She took it, letting him help her stand.

"Who do you think?" he asked. He saw Anana's blank, shocked face. "The board—who else? Listen, it's just my job, all right."

He pulled something out of his pocket, a net, which he began to unravel. "We were waiting for the first big snow fall. Did you get the pups collared?"

"No," Davis replied, looking where the wolves had disappeared. "Not yet. You may just have ruined my opportunity."

Tom was slipping the net under the wolf. "The other adults are wearing collars. We'll find them."

"You tracked them." Anana whispered her realization with dawning horror. The tent might have helped him find his mark, but it wasn't how he'd found the wolves in the first place. Tom began dragging the wolf through the snow toward his plane. "You used those collars to track them!"

Davis squeezed her hand. She worked for the Conservation only as a contractor on an as-needed basis, but she knew Davis worked for them full-time. She turned to him. "Did you know about this?"

"I have nothing to do with this," he told her, shaking his head. "Predator control has been taken out of our hands. Now guys like Tom work for the government and thin the population whenever they feel it's necessary."

"How can this be possible?" She shook her head and sank back to her knees in the snow. She touched the place were Amaguq had lain, the imprint of his body still fresh.

"I don't know," Davis replied, kneeling beside her and pulling her against him.

She rested her head against his shoulder, watching the small plane take off, the great black wolf tucked into the hull, already growing cold. Anana watched it until it grew to a small, black dot, letting Davis rock her. In the distance, they both heard the lamenting chorus of a pack of mourning wolves.

Author's Note:

In 2003, a law was passed in Alaska allowing aerial hunting of wolves for the first time in fifteen years. Governor Frank Murkowski and the Alaska Board of Game claimed that the killing of wolves was necessary from the air in order to boost game populations, such as moose and caribou. The law removed the Alaska Department of Fish and Game's final approval for implementing predator control and left the sole authority up to the Alaska Board of Game, who represent the Alaska Trappers Association and the extremist hunters of the Alaska Outdoor Council. A temporary restraining order seeking to halt Alaska's aerial gunning programs was denied by the Alaska Supreme Court on February 10th, 2006. Alaska governor and now vice-presidential candidate Sarah Palin added the incentive of a $150 bounty for any hunter who presented a wolf's foreleg. This means that the state's aerial gunning programs are once again in full swing and will continue through the end of April. More than 600 wolves have been killed over the past three winters and the new plans target approximately 600 more.

Law of Conservation

It had been threatening rain for days. Jeannie found her hand on the cradle of the old yellow phone on the wall even before it rang, staring out the kitchen window at the leaves turning up, showing their undersides in the wind. The barn cats had been cleaning themselves like mad, mewing plaintively just before sunset for two nights, as if they knew what was coming. There weren't many mosquitoes left in the season, but those that buzzed about flew low and bit hard. Ron's ankles were full of angry red bumps whenever he came in from the fields.

"Storm's coming your way!" Sally's voice crackled through the receiver, sounding far away, and she was. A thousand miles at least, and it felt like two.

"There's been a ring around the moon for two nights." Jeannie cradled the phone against her shoulder and reached for the towel she had been using to dry their dinner dishes. "Ron's out there battening everything down now."

"I saw it on the weather channel." Sally went on as if she hadn't heard, and Jeannie knew she probably hadn't. Her older sister liked to hear her own self talk more than anything else. "Looks real bad to your west on that Doppler thingie. You better make sure everything's tied down real good."

Jeannie slid a newly dried plate—mama's blue cornflowers were fading around the edges, but they were still pretty and more than serviceable—onto the top of the stack. With just the two of them, she only did dishes once a day, leaving them accumulating in the sink from breakfast until after they'd had supper.

"Did you say there was a ring around the moon?" Sally asked suddenly, interrupting herself.

"Yep." Jeannie leaned over the sink on tiptoes, looking for her husband, but she couldn't see anything except the cornfields to her left and the endless stretch of dying wildflowers and brush to her right. He wouldn't be out that way anyway, not out past the creek and up toward the towering power lines that stretched forever in both directions to the west of their farm. She saw steel girders rising web-like from ground to sky, like rows of towering metal monsters walking the earth, linked together, chain-gang style. She put her hand protectively over the little mound of tummy below her navel and turned away from the window with a shiver.

"Isn't that what Daddy always used to say?" Sally gave a short laugh and Jeannie smiled. Her sister had been gone away long enough to forget all the little things about living in the country, so when they came back, they were surprising and sweet, like the taste of a ripe peach just picked from the tree.

"Ring around the moon, storm's coming soon." They both repeated it at once, and Jeannie felt a flood of warmth, remembering stormy late night whisperings 'til morning in her sister's narrow bed. Sally had always been afraid of storms, but she pretended not to be. Jeannie kept up the pretense, feigning her own fear and climbing in to keep her sister company as lightning and thunder rocked their attic bedroom.

Audrey slept there, too, in that very bed.

Jeannie tried to push the unbidden thought back, along with the image of her daughter curled up, thumb half in half out of her mouth, her lower lip still moving as if she were sucking it in her sleep.

"So are you and Ron coming out in February for the reunion?"

"Sal—"

"I'm sending you plane tickets." Her sister's voice had that firm tone it always got when she was determined to get her own way.

"Don't."

"Yes, Jeannie." Sally's voice crackled again and Jeannie startled when lightning lit up the darkening sky.

"Please, don't." *One, two, three...* she counted the seconds between the flash and a loud clap of thunder that followed out of habit.

"Audrey isn't coming back."

The words startled her and Jeannie looked at the phone with its rotary dial and fat, buttery yellow casing, faded and cracked with age. "It's not that."

Sally went on, just like she always did. "I'm just saying... you two... I mean, you're still young, Jeannie. There's still time. You need to let life move on, you know?"

"It is." Jeannie smiled, her fingertips drumming on the tightening expanse of flesh below her navel, as if sending Morse code to the growing life inside as she leaned back against the counter. "Sally, I'm pregnant."

"You know, Mama always said—" Her sister's words stopped cold. "You're what?"

Jeannie tried not to laugh out loud. "I'm pregnant."

"Oh my god!" Sally's shriek was so loud Jeannie had to hold the phone out from her ear. "Oh my god, oh my god, oh my god!"

"I'm actually due right around February, so I think flying is going to be out of the question."

"That makes you..." Sally was clearly doing the math in her head and Jeannie waited, the grin stretching across her face so wide it almost hurt. "Almost four months along!? And you waited until now to tell me!?"

"Well, the tests kept coming up negative." Jeannie twirled the yellow cord around her finger, glancing out the kitchen window again and seeing the barn door swing open. "But the baby's growing, so the tests are obviously wrong."

She ignored the silence on the other end of the phone, watching her husband latch the barn door closed. He stopped to squint up at the sky, his hands on his hips, and the sight of him made her breath catch. "Listen, Sal, Ron's coming in. I have to go."

"Jeannie, wait!" Her sister didn't sound happy anymore. "Have you told him yet?"

"Not yet." She didn't wait for any response. "Bye, Sal." She walked over and hung the phone up on the ancient silver cradle just as Ron opened the back door, shaking off the first droplets of rain.

"Who was that?" His boots left muddy prints on the hardwood floor as he crossed over to the sink to wash his hands. He looked out her kitchen window, and she saw him nodding his head, *one, two,* after lightning flashed, counting the seconds just like she had. *It's close,* she thought.

"Just Sally." Jeannie watched him dry his hands on her damp dish towel. "Wanted to tell us she saw the storm coming on CNN."

He shook his head. "Don't need CNN to tell me that."

"No." Jeannie agreed as he grabbed a chair and sat down, leaning over to unlace his boots. "She also wants us to come to the family reunion in February."

Ron's fingers stopped unlacing and he glanced up at her, holding onto the lip of his baseball cap as he slid it back to scratch his dark head. "What'd you tell her?"

Jeannie shrugged, crossing her arms over her chest and leaning over the counter to look out the window again. At the edge of the field, the sun was sinking fast. It looked like a bleeding insect caught in the web of one of the power lines. The sky was growing darker overhead and lighting flashed again. There was no time to count, though, because a loud clap of thunder followed it almost immediately.

"I don't know if I can."

Ron just nodded, tossing his hat on the table and leaning over again to finish unlacing his boots. She watched him, thinking about the baby and wondering what he would say when she told him. This one would be a boy, she was sure of it, dark haired like his father with the same quick, lopsided smile and his broad hands with their wide nails. Jeannie drifted over, getting her bare knees dirty as she pulled up her long, soft brown skirt to kneel on the muddy floor in front of him. He leaned back and watched as she finished unlacing his boots, pulling them off and setting them aside.

She noticed a hole in his gray sock. "Have to darn that."

"I darn thee!" he joked, pointing at his heel and giving her that lopsided smile.

She returned his smile, shaking her head as she leaned her arms against his thighs, settling herself between them. "Goofball."

"I try." He tucked long, stray blonde hairs behind her ear, the same ones that always fell out of what he called "the-mommy-ponytail" she pulled her hair back into every morning. He'd stopped calling it that, though, since Audrey...

Outside the storm was beginning in earnest, and Jeannie jumped as a flash of lightning and a clap of thunder shook the house simultaneously. She wrapped her arms around her husband's waist, feeling his hands moving over her back as she rested her head in his lap.

"Do you like being a farmer?"

His fingers tangled in her hair. "I don't hate it."

"But?"

"You know." He pulled on her Scrunchie, spilling her hair over her shoulders.

"I guess."

His fingers massaged her scalp. "I just think there're too many memories here."

"For you?" She lifted her face to his, turning to rub her cheek against the palm of his hand.

He shook his head, running his thumb slowly over her lower lip. "For you."

"I like the memories." She kissed his palm.

"I just don't know if they like you."

The quality of the light in the kitchen moved from the fading edge of sunset toward darkness, and the storm outside was coming in, full force. She felt it in her belly, a low thrum, like something alive.

Jeannie nuzzled his hand out of the way, rubbing her cheek against the seam of his jeans, feeling him jump in surprise. "Well, *I* like *you*, Mr. Thomas."

"Sure about that?" He shifted his hips forward in the chair as she continued to graze her cheek against his crotch, feeling the slow hardening of his cock against the denim.

"You want proof?" His zipper ticked down easily between her fingers, and she undid the button of his jeans so she could caress him through his boxers, her lips running along his length over the material. His eyes were surprised, but pleased.

He smiled as she tugged on his jeans and he lifted his hips to accommodate her. "A man needs a little reassurance now and then."

"A little?" she teased, freeing him from his boxers now, too, rubbing the head against her open mouth and flattened tongue, her eyes on his.

"A little more..." he urged, his hand fisted in her hair as he pressed her down on him, easing his cock slowly between her lips. "Ahhhh yeah... more..."

Jeannie couldn't talk to tease him anymore, so she used her tongue to do the job, rolling it around the head as she came up on him and then slid down again, wetting the length of his shaft with her saliva. Ron's hands moved to the sides of the chair, gripping the edges as she began to suck him urgently, thrusting his hips up to meet her motion.

The sound of the storm filled her ears as her husband's cock filled her mouth, the light fading quickly to gray shadow as the sky darkened with rain. Water flooded from the sky in a deluge, sheeting against the windows and making rippling patterns on their faces. Jeannie took him into her mouth as far as she could, whimpering with her yearning for more as he rocked upward on the chair, his head thrown back in pleasure.

She would have stayed there, eager for him to burst in her mouth like the thunderheads soaking the rich, dark earth, but he used his grip on her hair to ease her off his cock with a thick pop. There was only a moment of eye contact before he pulled her up to him, his hungry mouth on hers, greedy hands pushing her skirt high and nestling the taut crotch of her panties against his erection.

Jeannie slid herself against the length of his cock, moaning when his tongue found its way into her mouth, teasing her, flickering over her lips before sinking deep in exploration again. His hands gripped her behind, rocking the chair back onto two legs as she ground her hips in circles against him, hooking her feet around his calves to give her more leverage.

"Easy, easy," he murmured as the chair slid back further, threatening to tip over entirely. "We're not exactly stable, here."

She gripped the table for balance and stood, turning so she could slide her bottom up over the edge. He watched as she spread her legs and pulled her skirt up to reveal herself to him as she laid back on the hard surface. "Better?"

"Almost." He turned his chair toward her, hooking his thumbs in her panties and pulling them down her thighs. Then he leaned in to taste her, parting the curly blonde hair between her legs with his tongue. The soft press of his lips against her clit made her shiver and she moaned when he asked, "See, isn't that better?"

"Much!" She gasped when his fingers eased between her lips, parting them, searching the wet, pinks folds until he found what he wanted. Spreading her legs wider, she lifted her hips to meet the thrust of his fingers easing in and out of her flesh. His tongue was like a hot pulse on her clit and it excited her even more when she recognized the telltale, rhythmic motion between her legs that meant he was stroking himself as he licked her.

Jeannie cupped her breasts, rubbing her palms against the hardening of her nipples under the material. Shadows quivered across the ceiling, reflected from the kitchen window as the storm raged outside. The thunder was coming hard and fast after each flash of lightning—no longer a distant rumble, it shook the house like an explosion every few minutes. It went through her body, electric, as if she were a conduit and her husband's flickering tongue a hot, live wire.

"Oh god, Ronnie!" She lifted her hips to meet his plunging fingers and lashing tongue, her orgasm coming in like the rain, fast and hard and without mercy. It shook her as the house trembled against the storm, and she grabbed fistfuls of her skirt as she came, stretching the material taut over her contracting lower belly as her body twisted and shuddered on the table. Ronnie gave a low groan as she flooded his tongue with her juices, the motion between his legs so rapid it rattled her on the surface of the table along with the after-dinner coffee cups and saucers she hadn't cleared.

Ron's mouth moved over her mound, kissing, leisurely, deliciously over her swollen lips, pressing her thighs back with open palms. She gasped and twisted as he flicked his tongue teasingly over her sensitive clit and then began to kiss his way up toward her belly. Jeannie reacted quickly then, sliding down off the table and turning around, pulling her skirt high up over her hips as she bent over the table.

Her husband groaned when she reached back and used both hands to open herself for him. It wasn't completely dark yet, and she knew he must be able to see the glistening spread of her pussy, the dark, puckered hole of her ass—the look of lust in his eyes as he stood up behind her with the thick length of his cock gripped tightly in his fist was proof enough.

"Do you want that?" she whispered, arching her back and tilting her hips as she looked over her shoulder at him, inching her fingers inward toward her swollen labia, parting them further. "Are you hard for that, baby?"

He split her pussy lips even more with the fat head of his cock and Jeannie sighed with satisfaction as he slipped it up and down the slick cleft, seeking the path of least resistance and finding it with a shift of his hips. His hands moved to grip her behind as he sank his length slowly into her, and she moaned at the sensation, going up on her bare toes to give him even deeper access.

Resting her cheek against the smooth surface of the table, Jeannie waited, breathless, for him to continue, to begin to fuck her in earnest, but he held himself there, throbbing and buried inside of her. She felt the bite of his zipper against the back of her thighs, his jeans still only halfway down, and it thrilled her to know they had gone from everyday chit chat and the removal of his muddy boots to her bent over the kitchen table with her skirt up around her waist and his cock buried in to the hilt in the space of a few minutes.

"Do you feel that?" he murmured, kneading her flesh with his thumbs, prying her apart as if trying to find more flesh to sink further into.

Jeannie opened her mouth to say something affirmative, aching to feel him thrust, her clit, still throbbing from her climax, hungry for more—but then she *did* feel something. Something else, something besides the sweet sensation of their joined bodies, hips pressed tightly together. It filled the air, like some sort of static electricity, making her skin tingle and the hair on the back of her neck stand up.

"Ron?" She turned her head back to look at him with puzzled eyes and knitted brow, and that's when it happened.

Jeannie hadn't turned the lights on in the kitchen before the storm began—she'd always been careful about using electricity sparingly in the house, a holdover from her father's frugal "Were you raised in a barn?" lectures—but there was always a little night light plugged in above the toaster in case one of them came down in the middle of the night, and when lightning flashed outside, it suddenly flickered and burned brightly hot for a moment, a thrumming sound filling the air, followed by a little pop and a fizzle. She didn't know if it was her imagination, but she thought she could smell something burning.

Ron groaned, moving to slide out of her, but she reached her hand back, grabbing his thigh and digging her nails in. "No!"

"It's a blackout, I think," he panted, "Maybe the little generator out back got hit or something..."

"So fuck me in the dark." She slid her hand between her thighs, feeling the weight of his balls as she nudged them out of the way to find her clit. "Just... fuck... me!" She punctuated each word with a squeeze of her pussy and Ron gasped at the sensation, his hands tightening on her ass.

"Jeannie, I really should—"

"Fuck me!" she insisted, thrusting back on him, moving her pussy over the length of his cock. It took her a moment to catch a rhythm as she rubbed her clit in fast circles, her hardened nipples grazing the table through the light material of her shirt. With a low grunt, her husband relented and began to move, shoving her against the table and driving in deep.

"Yes!" Jeannie rubbed herself, moaning at the delicious, added sensation of Ron's balls slapping against her hand that worked fast and hard between her legs as he began to fuck her hard. They were in almost total darkness now except for the brief flashes of lightning as she twisted and bucked beneath him on the table. He half leaned over her, now, lost in his own ride toward climax, making thrilling little grunting noises with every thrust that made her shiver with lust.

"Ronnie," she warned, knowing he liked to hear her just before, to know she was about to come, knowing, too, that it would push him further toward his own orgasm. "I'm so close, so close..."

"Come on, baby," he urged, rolling his hips now, slowing, and she knew he was drawing it out for himself, making it last, keeping himself hovering on that quivering edge, and that pushed her over. "Come all over me."

"Nnnnnnnng!" She bit her own arm as she felt the rise of her climax and worked toward it. "Ohhh fuck, baby, yes! You want me to come all over that hard cock? You want my little pussy to come all over you?"

Ron groaned at her words, slowing his movements even further, but Jeannie was lost, going, gone with it, her hand and swollen pussy lips soaking wet with her juices as she ground her fingers against the bud of her clit.

"Now!" She gasped, arching, everything in her body taut as she went sliding over that slippery edge, letting herself fully go onto the table, her feet off the ground as Ron reached around to grab her thighs and shove himself deep into her pussy. He leaned into her, biting her back, her shoulder as he shuddered against her, and she felt the deep throb in her belly as he came, too.

"Fuck!" He staggered against her, no longer in control, shoving the table and the chair tucked underneath it back against the wall. Jeannie's quivering pussy worked around his cock and she made unconscious circles with her hips as she came, squeezing him uncontrollably, feeling every inch of his length pulsing with his climax. An incredible heat filled her belly as they both succumbed, their bodies still contracting with pleasure as they both collapsed into a heap on the kitchen table.

Conscious of the weight of her husband's body now, Jeannie squirmed beneath him, gasping, moving to protect her lower belly and the baby growing there. Ron acquiesced, sitting back shakily in the chair waiting behind him, his pants falling around his ankles. Jeannie picked her panties up off the floor with a smile, dropping them on the table behind her as she stood.

"Wow... what was that all about?" Ron straightened his legs and hitched his pants up, keeping his hips lifted until he could button them.

She shrugged, still smiling. "The storm, I guess."

"I wonder if I can cut a deal with the weather man?"

"I think you'd have to consult with someone a little higher up." Jeannie nodded toward the kitchen window, the smile fading from her face as the thunderous sound of hail started outside. It sounded like thousands of stones being dropped from the sky onto the roof. She gasped, grabbing for Ron, and he stood, pulling her with him toward the window. They stood holding onto each other in front of the sink, watching fat, rounded pieces of ice bouncing off the grass and the roof of the barn.

"The animals?" Jeannie asked, wincing at the sound of the hail hitting the roof.

"They're all in." His voice was reassuring as he kissed the top of her head.

"Let's go to bed."

He laughed. "It's only seven-thirty."

"I know." She reached around, grabbing a handful of flesh underneath the seat of his jeans.

He jumped, eyes widening. "Oh."

"Race ya."

* * * *

Jeannie rolled toward her husband in the dark, hearing his deep, even breathing, but knowing he wasn't quite asleep yet. After ten years of sleeping next to the same person, you learned all their noises—even the pretend ones. He wanted her to believe he was asleep, was perhaps convincing himself he was almost there, but he wasn't.

"I had a dream about Audrey last night."

Outside, the rain continued, although the hail had stopped even before they reached the bedroom, and the lightning and thunder were nowhere near as furious as they had been. Ron's breathing didn't change, and he didn't answer. The lights hadn't come back on yet. The digital clocks in the nightstands were both still dark, and she had no idea what time it was, but guessed it around David Letterman time.

"Was that what you were dreaming about when I brought you back to bed the last time?" He gave up the pretense and turned toward her.

"Yes." She smiled, sliding her thigh up over his. The slick feel of his cum between her pussy lips was warm and sticky. It had been a long time since they'd spent a night like this. "I haven't dreamed about her in months."

"Something keeps getting you out of bed." Ron slipped an arm behind her back and pulled her closer. She snuggled in, thinking of Audrey, wondering how to segue into telling him about the new baby. "I keep finding you trying to open the back door."

She'd been sleepwalking since just after Audrey died. They'd spent those last weeks in the hospital, hoping the "final treatment option" would be successful. Jeannie didn't sleep much then—and when she did, it was awkward, in strange positions in uncomfortable chairs, or curled around Audrey's emaciated frame when she called for mommy in the middle of the night, trying to comfort without hurting, without putting any weight on her little girl's delicate, aching bones. The leukemia had spread to her liver by then, tingeing the whites of her eyes yellow with that gold ringed dot of cornflower blue in their centers. They stared out of sunken hollows, pleading for something. Release? Jeannie didn't think she could ever let her go.

But I did.

They had come home to the farm without her. No more Audrey running around the yard chasing chickens, pulling the barn cats' tails, tearing up and down the gravel driveway on her training wheels. They had come home from the funeral, just the two of them, and Jeannie had never left it again. Not to go shopping, not to visit neighbors, not even to the hospital when Ron hurt his hand last fall cutting wood for the winter. She had come home." and slept—all day, all night—curled up in bed, or in front of a fire in the living room, or on the front porch swing wrapped in a blanket. She was sleeping awake, or awake sleeping, all the time it felt like. That state of consciousness had morphed slowly, over time, but the sleepwalking had never really stopped. It just happened at night, now, when Ron found her pounding on the back door, or hiding in the pantry, afraid of some unknown subconscious monster.

Some part of me wants out. That seemed true enough, considering she hadn't left the house in two years. Lately, she always ended up bumping into or knocking on their back door in her sleep. "It's a good thing I can't seem to work all those locks while I'm dreaming."

Ron snorted, shaking his head. He had put extra locks on when Audrey was really little and had learned how to manipulate the ones on the handles. Paranoid about the creek out back, Jeannie had insisted. Now they had five locks a piece on each door, as if they lived in some inner city instead of out in the middle of nowhere.

"What did you dream?" he asked.

Jeannie hesitated, blinking in the darkness. "I dreamed about a storm."

"She was so afraid of storms." Ron's arm tightened around her shoulder.

Jeannie closed her eyes, remembering, hearing Audrey's plaintive cry, rushing up the cold, wooden stairs on bare feet. It seemed so real because it had been. "I went up to the attic to comfort her. But she wasn't there."

"That explains what you were doing up there."

"I've had that dream over and over... hearing her crying, going up to look for her, and not finding her there." Jeannie's eyes filled with tears and she felt Ron's lips press against her forehead.

"She's still here, baby."

"No, she isn't!"

"Maybe not the way we remember her." She hated how calm he sounded, like he'd come to some sort of peace with it all. "But you know what they say about energy... it can't be created or destroyed, right? It can only change form."

"Whatever." Jeannie swallowed around the lump in her throat.

"I still feel her here. Don't you?"

"Only when I'm dreaming." She remembered Ron shaking her after the dream, leading her back to their bed. "Anyway, she wasn't there, but I could hear her... she was talking to me."

"What'd she say?"

The lie came easily: "I don't remember."

"Yes you do."

"It was nothing." She rolled away from him, hugging her pillow to her. She didn't like telling him about what happened in her dreams. She didn't like telling anyone about them. "Something about wires. Alivewires."

"Live wires?" Ron leaned over her, and she could hear his frown.

"*Alive*wires."

"Those fucking things." He rolled away from her, too, jostling the bed and leaving a half foot space between them that felt enormous.

"Ronnie..." Now was the time to tell him. *We're going to have a baby.* It would make it all better, and the argument rising between them like some hot, electrical storm would dissipate as if it had never been. Why couldn't she say the words?

He turned to her first, closing the gap, pulling her around to face him. "Let's go, Jeannie. We can move anywhere you want. How about out to Colorado where Sally is? Wouldn't you like that?"

"I can't." She shook her tousled blonde head in the dark, twisting away from him. "This is my home. This is our farm. My parents lived here their *whole lives.*"

"Some life." Ron tucked his arms behind his head and stared at the ceiling. "Mommy dies of breast cancer, daddy follows with a brain tumor. They never even lived long enough to see their own granddaughter."

"Oh, right, here we go again"

"What?"

"The cancer gene." Jeannie's voice trembled. "It's all my fault."

He sighed. "Remember what Dr. Sullivan told us about those fucking monster power lines we live next door to? *They make the cancer grow.*"

"Dr. Sullivan!" She laughed, a high, strangled sound. "Oh, please! Let's bow down to the Dr. Guru of Incense and Organic Diets. He thought *breathing* made cancer grow."

"I don't want to have this argument anymore."

"Well, if we'd taken her to a real doctor, instead of that alternative medicine quack, she might just still be here!"

"That's not fair." Ron's voice cracked.

"Tell me about it."

They both rolled over toward their night stands, the digital clocks on each now blinking 12:00. Power's back, Jeannie thought, pulling the blanket over her bare shoulder. The silence stretched, and eventually, she heard Ron's low snore and knew he was really asleep. *So much for my good news.* She got up to pee, going into the bathroom attached to their bedroom, but not turning on the light, afraid to wake him. Outside, she knew the moon was full, but still hidden behind storm clouds, the rain falling steadily on the roof.

She wiped herself, pulling the tissue out to look as she always did, a life time of habit. A brief flash of lightning showed a dark spot on the white paper and her heart skipped at the sight of it. *Blood?* Closing the door, she turned on the light and stared down at the red streak.

It's just from sex, she reassured herself, dropping the offending tissue into the toilet and flushing it away. Her hands were shaking, though, when she washed them, and it felt like a long time before she actually fell into sleep after slipping a t-shirt over her head and crawling in next to her husband in bed.

* * * *

i'm alive i'm alive i'm alive

She's gone, Jeannie. She's not coming back. Nothing can bring her back.

i'm here right here mommy look look catch me

You need to get on with your life. You need to move forward.

so fast silver fast mommy lightfast can you see me look look

Wake up! Wake up!

look up! look up!

She's not here. Don't kid yourself. It's a dream. You're dreaming.

here here i'm here here in the wires the wires alivewires herewires alivewires

You watched her die. You let her take her last breath.

come with me come with me here mommy look up fastwires alivewires upwires

Stay with me. Stay with me.

alivewires alivewires alivewires alivewires...

Jeannie jolted awake, moaning in the darkness and rubbing the place where her forehead had collided with something hard and rather sharp. She could still feel a thick vibration in her head, like a tuning fork that had been struck, and she put both hands on either side as if she could stop the sensation.

"Ron!" Her voice was nothing but a croak and she groped forwardly blindly with her hands, her eyes not adjusted yet. She realized she had been sleepwalking, but it took her a moment to come to grips with her bodily sensations mixed with the fading images of her dream. "Ron!"

She blinked, her fingers wet with something sticky, and understood suddenly her forehead was bleeding. Swiping at the wound, she pressed her palm there, her eyes searching her surroundings in the limited light. *Outside. I'm outside.* She remembered falling asleep, Ron snoring beside her, the sound of the rain on the roof. No one had locked up after they'd gone upstairs to bed. The myriad of locks on the doors had been open, and she had sleepwalked right out into the darkness.

Panicked, she blinked and squinted, looking for something familiar, the warm, square lights of the house *(Is the power back on? The power came back on, didn't it?)* or the silhouette of the weather vane on top of the barn. The darkness, however, was complete. There was nothing to light her way, no landmark building she could discern. The rain had stopped, but the ground was wet and cold beneath her bare feet and legs, the grass of the field she was standing in at least knee high. She took a step forward and winced at the dull ache in her feet, as if she had been walking a long time. A long time.

She hugged herself, shivering in just a white t-shirt that barely covered her behind, wondering what to do next. Ron would come looking for her—but when he found she wasn't in the house, which way would he go? Which way had she gone? Should she stay put and wait until the cavalry arrived with a flashlight and a blanket to escort her home?

Daddy always said, if you get lost in the woods, stay put, she remembered, checking the bleeding on her forehead. It seemed to have slowed. What had she cut herself on? Turning, she saw the faint outline of a steel girder, and she touched it in the darkness. *The power lines.*

Since before she could remember, their farm had been bordered by the local power company's land where these metal monsters stretched out their wide arms, linked together with thick cables toward their narrowed tips, their triangular bases a solid webbing of steel.

Stay put, unless you know exactly where you are. But she did know, didn't she? If she followed the seemingly endless row of power lines, it would lead her right back to the house. *But I don't know which direction I'm headed.* That was true, but it didn't matter. Eventually, the power lines would cross a road. She could follow the road to a house. Someone's house, some place warm with a phone. Leaning against the steel beam, she considered her options, shifting from side to side in the wet grass, still hugging herself, this time for warmth instead of from fear.

Glancing up at the sky, she saw nothing but clouds moving in the darkness. No moon, no stars to guide by to tell her direction. *To hell with it, I'm going home.* Staying out here, cold and shivering in the dark, bleeding from the forehead *(blood? Do you remember blood?)* and four months pregnant on top of it was tantamount to craziness. She'd lived out here all her life—she trusted her body to know which way to go. She started walking, careful to keep the faint outline of the power lines stretched above her head and one steel beast to her front and to her back.

* * * *

It felt as if she'd been walking for hours, and yet there was nothing but the field and the row of power lines stretching into darkness. Jeannie collapsed beside a steel beam, exhausted, ignoring the thick, wet grass, her feet already numb, her legs shivering with cold. She hugged her knees and rocked, closing her eyes and humming to herself. It was a song she used to sing to Audrey. Sally taught it to her in that little narrow bed when the storms came and rocked the old farm house like a giant nudging a toy.

"I used to know the words." She said this out loud, teeth chattering, glancing up at the sky as drops of rain started to fall.

sing me the song mommy the one about home

Jeannie rocked, trying to remember, the rain coming down harder now, moving from sprinkle to drizzle.

we know it we know it come home come home

She glanced up to the sky, rain falling on her face, and finally understood where the words were coming from, where they had been coming from since Audrey had gone. The dreams, the words, the whispers, the walks, they all ended here, right here, the center of everywhere and nowhere all at once. Standing, Jeannie turned toward the huge, steel frame, and heard a whispered hiss:

Yesssss

She gripped the edges of the cold, slippery metal in her hands, putting one bare foot on the cross beam and started to climb.

Alivealivealivewiresalivewires

Glancing up, she saw the taut cables, humming with life, whispering to her, calling her. *home home home* Jeannie's feet slid across the metal post and she gasped, gripping the bar above her head, which was just as slippery. The rain made it a slick climb and she had little traction, but already she had pulled herself up past the first tier.

The humming was louder, now, and she reached for the next bar, continuing to climb. She smiled as she remembered Sally singing the song, Sally who had been like a mother after her own mother was gone, the last song Jeannie had sung to her baby as she rocked her to sleep for the very last time.

Jeannie sang:
"I gaze on the moon
As I tread the drear wild
And feel that my mother
Now thinks of her child..."*

Above her, the clouds parted, revealing the haloed moon and illuminating everything around her. She was pulling up past the second tier now, breathing hard, and saw the moonlight on the wet grass below her, the reflection of the rain like silver on the steel webbing under her feet.

She sang as she climbed, higher into the night, toward the moon, the one that had been forecasting storms for days.

"As she looks on that moon
From our own cottage door,
Thro' the woodbine whose fragrance
Shall cheer me no more..."*

Across the field, each steel edifice seemed to glow in the moonlight, as if lighting her way, making a path toward home. She thought she could see the faint outline of the house, now, the dark hulk of the barn behind it—and a low beam of light moving across the ground towards her.

Jeannie continued to climb. The third tier narrowed and gave way to a steeper structure, her feet finding places closer together to step as she neared the top. The low hum she heard on the ground was louder here, more distinct. Now there were words, a low communication, a whisper, a sigh, like breath against her face as she moved closer to the source.

"*Home, home, sweet sweet home,*
There's no place like home,
There's no place like home..."*

The cool air filled her lungs as she took one last shaky step toward the very top of the structure. She'd never felt so alive.

i'm alive i'm alive i'm alive
She's gone, Jeannie. She's not coming back. Nothing can bring her back.
i'm here right here mommy look look catch me
You need to get on with your life. You need to move forward.
so fast silver fast mommy lightfast can you see me look look

"Jeannie!"

The voice came from below her, but she was listening to the ones from above. They seemed to come from everywhere. It was Audrey's voice, small and light and full of brightness, but it was more. She was more. And she was here, right here, all along.

Wake up! Wake up!
look up! look up!

"I am up, baby." Jeannie reached out to touch one of the cables, thick and hard, not rubbery as she imagined, and thought she felt it thrumming in her hand.

"Jeannie!" It was Ron, waving a flashlight far down below. He looked so small. He felt so small. Up here, she was bigger than everything.

She's not here. Don't kid yourself. It's a dream. You're dreaming.

here here i'm here here in the wires the wires alivewires herewires alivewires

"I feel you." She did. It was glorious.

You watched her die. You let her take her last breath.

come with me come with me here mommy look up fastwires alivewires upwires

"Jeannie! What are you doing!?"

"Going home," she whispered, blinking back tears, but for the first time in years, she didn't feel sad.

"Come down!" His voice was louder, and she glanced down, seeing him putting his foot on the first cross bar. "Okay, stay right there! I'm coming up."

Stay with me. Stay with me.

alivewires alivewires alivewires alivewires...

"I'm coming." They were the last words she said as she swung out onto the cable. Both of her hands lost their grip on the slippery surface. It happened almost instantly, and she quickly descended the deadly distance to the ground.

* * * *

Ron stared at the broken yellow casing of the phone, listening to his sister-in-law's voice crackle through the line.

"I don't understand." Sally sobbed, making Ron close his eyes against it. "If it had been just after... I mean... she had so much to live for..."

"The funeral's Friday.

Sally sniffed. "Did she tell you, Ron?"

"Tell me what?"

The silence stretched and she took a deep breath. "About the baby?"

"What baby?" Ron leaned back against the counter, watching the sun set through the steel girders across the field through the kitchen window. The sight of it filled him with a murderous rage.

"Oh god." Sally's voice was barely audible. "She was pregnant, Ron. She told me she was about four months pregnant."

"No." He shook his head, incredulous, understanding more than he wanted to, his eyes following the webbing upward to the narrowing top of the tower. "She wasn't pregnant, Sal. It was a tumor. The autopsy showed it probably started as ovarian cancer. But they told me she wouldn't have lived through the winter. It was everywhere."

*Home, Sweet Home
Traditional
Written By: John H. Payne
Music By: Henry R. Bishop

Author's Note:

Although numerous studies have produced contradictory results, many experts are absolutely convinced the threat of electromagnetic fields (EMF) is quite real.

According to one study, "People who lived within 328 yards of a power line up to the age of five were five times more likely to develop cancer. Those who lived within the same range to a power line at any point during their first 15 years were three times more likely to develop cancer as an adult."

By 1990, over a hundred studies had been conducted worldwide. Of these, at least two dozen studies on humans indicated a link between EMF's and health issues.

Even the Environmental Protection Agency (EPA) issued warnings, stating, "There is reason for concern" and advised "prudent avoidance."

Originally, the EPA recommended that EMF's be classified as a Class B carcinogen—a "probable human carcinogen," joining the ranks of formaldehyde, DDT, dioxins, and PCB's.

However, once the EPA's draft report was released, utility, military, and computer lobbyists fought and won— their final revision ended up not classifying EMF's as a Class B carcinogen. Rather, the following explanation was added: "At this time such a characterization regarding the link between cancer and exposure to EMF's is not appropriate because the basic nature of the interaction between EMF's and biological processes leading to cancer is not understood."

Sources: Pub Med Study, Dr. Mercola

Lightning Doesn't Strike Twice

The morning light was different when it came into our windows on that side of the house now. Rusty said I was crazy. The grass all grew back, but I kept telling him, if you put down enough hydroseed and mulch, you could grow grass on asphalt if you wanted to. That's pretty much what they did.

"People could die." I heard myself mumbling when he came to me. I was only half awake.

"You're dreaming again, Erin Brockovich." Rusty kissed my temple as he slid into bed, nudging Domino out of the way. Domino lifted his big black and white Great Dane head and snorted, edging down to the bottom of the bed and curling up where Scrabble, our Benji-faced mutt, liked to keep my feet warm at night.

"Very funny." I stretched and rolled toward Rusty, snuggling my sleep-warmed body next to his freshly showered one. I never understood his taking a shower before going down into the mines to get filthy again. "People really could die."

"Everyone's gonna die, Lolly." He kissed my forehead. "Might as well die a good death. What should we die from?"

"I don't want to die."

He chuckled. "I don't think that's an option."

"Have a good day." I kissed his cheek, closing my eyes again and settling back into my pillow.

"Oh, I'm not leaving yet..." His hand slipped under the covers, seeking the silky softness of my nightgown. "I don't even have my socks on."

I cocked one eye half open at him. "You woke me up and you don't even have your socks on?"

"I'm being selfish today." He grinned. "You're the one thing that gets me through the day, you know."

"Is that so?"

His fingers edged the material up my thigh. "Unfortunately, it ends up being a one-to-one ratio... one minute with you, one hour in the pit."

"Aww." I moved back toward him, slipping my arms around his neck and massaging the muscles in his shoulders. "I know...you work so hard."

"Don't mind hard work." He gave a soft groan when my fingers dug into the tendons of his neck. "Damn, I'm never going to get my socks on at this rate. You're not helping."

I smiled. "Your feet are all the way down there."

"Funny girl."

"I try."

"It won't happen again, you know." Rusty's eyes closed as I massaged his shoulders through his t-shirt. "It's like lightning striking twice in the same place."

I shook my head, but knew he couldn't see me. "No, it's not like that at all."

"I'm more worried about dying of a heart attack."

"Then quit going to Taco Bell for lunch."

"Maybe it's because I'm going to be forty." He rolled his head around, groaning again as I dug my fingers deeper, the way I knew he liked. "It's good to be unhealthy at forty. Gives you something to do besides buy convertibles and cheat on your wife."

"You can have all the convertibles you want."

He snorted. "Yeah, Matchbox ones." There was a pause as I worked my fingers over his flesh. "What about the cheating on your wife part?"

"You can have all the convertibles you want," I repeated, squeezing his shoulders hard.

He grinned. "Oh, sure, I can have a *car* with the top down, but a woman—"

"You want a woman with her top down?" I slipped the black straps of my nightgown over my shoulders, wiggling it down to my navel.

Rusty's eyes lit up. "You're gonna make me late, woman..."

"So make it worth it." I reached for him and he came to me, burying his face between my breasts with a grin. I didn't mind a morning quickie, and I especially wanted one this morning, considering I knew we wouldn't see each other again for two more days. Our schedules were off for the rest of the week, and I knew I was ovulating. I'd just bought one of those little kits on the way home from work last week.

"Nowhere near hard enough," I murmured, feeling his cock at half-mast through his briefs. His tongue made wet circles over my nipples, first one, then the other, making them stand up pink and proud.

"Gonna have to do something about that then." His fingers replaced his tongue as he licked his way down my belly. I knew where he was headed and spread my legs, eager for his mouth. He liked to warm me up, and licking me always made him hard as a rock.

"Damn, you're wet." His eyes were bright as he sank his tongue between my shaved lips.

I gave him a secret smile. "I'm ovulating."

His eyebrows went up. "No pressure or anything."

"Don't you wanna make a baby?" I moaned when his fingers slid inside of me, his tongue teasing my clit.

"I told you I did." He kissed circles around it and then did the same with his tongue, making me dizzy with the pleasure of the motion. I gave up a soft cry to the ceiling, closing my eyes to the funny light that came in the window on that side of the house now, rocking my hips up to meet him. I knew his cock was growing hard against the mattress and I imagined it, long and thick and throbbing, aching to slide into my wetness.

"Rusty," I panted, grabbing his dark hair in my fists. "Come on. Put it in me."

"Don't you wanna come?" He lifted his wet face, wiping at his chin, and I smiled, tugging gently at his curls.

"I want *you* to come," I urged as he slid up between my thighs, slipping his underwear down his hips. I pressed my mouth to his ear, sucking at his earlobe and making him groan—he loved that so much—before reaching for his cock. It was just as I knew it would be, thick and pulsing in my hand, eager for my pussy. "I want you to come inside of me."

He groaned as I slid it between my lips. "It won't be long," he warned. Like I didn't know—it had been almost two weeks since we'd done it. Whenever we went so long, he came almost the minute he slid inside me. He always apologized, but I secretly loved how good it made him feel to be in me.

"Should I be mean?" I teased, rocking my hips up and sliding him in deep. I made my voice high and breathy. "Oh, baby, please don't come yet, it feels so good."

"Ohhh!" He bent his head to nip at my breast. "Brat!'

"Oh, Rusty, baby, please," I moaned, sliding my hands down his back, cupping his ass as he began to fuck me. "Don't come, please, I want to come first…"

"Quit." He leaned in and kissed me quiet, his tongue slipping between my lips, making me shiver. I loved the way he kissed me, the thousand ways he had of kissing me. His cock plunged with the same rhythm as his tongue and I wrapped my arms and legs around him, hanging on and enjoying the ride.

He broke the kiss, moaning into my mouth, "Ohhhh fuck, baby!" God, I loved hearing him like that, pushing toward the edge.

"Come on," I urged, reaching between us to feel his cock thrusting into me, rubbing my clit with my fingers. "Do it! Fuck me hard!"

He slipped his arms under me, his weight almost entirely on me, now, crushing the breath out of me, but I didn't care. I welcomed him, my hand working faster, rubbing myself toward the same end. God, he made me want to come so hard, his breath panting in my ear, his hips thrusting against mine, bodies slapping so hard the bed shook and made Domino whine and jump down to settle in a pile of dirty laundry on the floor.

"Rusty, I'm gonna come," I whispered, my eyes half-closing. He searched my face for the truth and saw it, groaning at the realization. My pussy clamped down on his shaft with that first shuddering wave and I bit his shoulder to keep from crying out—it always made Scrabble howl right along with me. Rusty drove in deep and fast, grunting as he came. I felt every hot throb of his cock as we trembled together. I don't know why, but I had tears in my eyes as I felt him filling me, again and again.

"I'm gonna be late." Rusty groaned as he rolled off me and out of bed, his hand searching the floor for his socks and underwear.

I smiled, still breathless, watching him pull them on. "You keep saying that."

"What are you gonna do today?" He stood, starting to slip his coveralls on.

"I have to update the web site before I go into the diner at four." I loved my late days, getting to laze in bed with the dogs.

"What about dinner?"

"I'll have something in the crock pot waiting for you, just like I always do on my late days, Mr. Spoiled Rotten."

He buttoned himself into his coveralls, picking up his keys from the bureau and pocketing them. "Can it please not have too many vegetables in it?"

"I thought you didn't want to die of a heart attack?" I smiled, rubbing my knees together under the covers, loving the feel of his cum on my thighs. *Maybe we made a baby.* I didn't want to say anything and jinx it, but I had a funny feeling. I wondered how the dogs would react when we finally had a little one...

"I don't—what the fuck is that?" Rusty turned toward the window, the one with the funny morning light. Domino's head shot up at the sound and he whined.

"Sounds like Clint shooting off his .22 at the coons again." I rolled to my back and put my knees up. That's what they said you should do at the web sites I'd been visiting in between working on the one for the Coldwater Creek Spill. All the trying-to-conceive sites (TTC, they called it—they had a whole language all their own) said it encouraged a "seminal pool" at the "opening of the cervix." Whatever might make us a baby, if it meant standing on my head, I was willing.

"Lolly." Rusty stood looking out the window, pushing the dog down. Domino wanted to see, too, but Scrabble barely lifted his head from his paws on the bed.

"What?"

"Lightning's striking twice in the same place."

I sat up, forgetting about semen and the possibility of babies. "Oh my god."

I ran to the window, hanging onto the ledge to see what Rusty was talking about. The sound hadn't been a gun. It was the trees. One after the other, they were cracking in half under the weight of the sludge.

"It's coming too fast." His voice sounded strangled, like he was already drowning in it. "It's gonna bury us."

"Oh my god."

He turned to me, pulling me into his arms. "We can't get out in time."

"Rusty!" I turned toward the window again, seeing a river of black flooding the creek bed. "We have to try!"

Rusty shook his head. His voice was barely audible. "Guess I'm not gonna die of a heart attack."

"This can't be happening." I stared at the mountain of waste, the stuff no one wanted to think about, the stuff they wanted to cover up, buried in the earth like a secret. There was no word for it—it was just the stuff that was leftover after the coal was washed, thick as molasses, a black freight train barreling down the mountainside. Everything behind it was dark. Familiar objects I'd seen a million times when I looked out that window, houses and trees, were simply gone, as if they'd been erased completely by the black torrent heading our way.

I could barely hear my own voice. "I have to update the web site."

"Lolly…"

I clutched his coveralls, freshly laundered but always dirty somehow. "I have to—"

"Shut up!" He shook me, hard, and I turned to him, seeing a shift of the light out of the corner of my eye, like the sun being blotted out—swallowed in blackness. He pressed his forehead to mine and croaked, "I love you."

I felt a sudden wetness between my legs as his semen slipped down my thigh in a thick flood. "I love you, too."

Author's Note:

At 12:30 in the morning of October 11, 2000, a mountain in eastern Kentucky burst open and let out a flood of mining waste bigger than the Exxon Valdez oil spill. Coal sludge damaged homes and killed everything in 20 miles of streams.

Reports say that there are seven hundred waste impoundments like the one that leaked in 2000 scattered throughout the mining regions. Other sources put the number at a thousand or more.

Source: On Earth Magazine

The Break

Fucking global warming.

Luke cursed it even as he enjoyed the fact that his fingers weren't numb without the gloves he had tucked into his pocket and his ass wasn't frozen to the platform. The blind was high and the deer were plentiful. Deer season had been over in Wisconsin for more than a month and the animals had stopped being so shy and ventured out much further. Still, he had to walk a mile in the dark to this blind, and there was the long climb up into the tree after that. His fifty year old body was much more unreliable that it should have been at his age, and he often wondered if he might just get stuck up there some day and freeze to death, only to be found half-eaten and thawing next spring by some hunter.

Not gonna freeze in these temperatures.

The season had been much too warm, and the deer were enjoying the breakthroughs in the ice at the edges where they could find fresh water. They were mostly does and their young, though, and Luke needed a buck. One with a big rack. *Speaking of racks...* He blew a low, misted breath out and shifted slightly. His left butt cheek was completely numb, not from cold but from sitting so long, and the sudden association of racks—*deer rack...Mia's rack*—had made an unexpected dent in the denim of his jeans.

Not gonna freeze, but not gonna get laid, either. Yeah, sure, it was a crude guy-thought... and he felt momentarily and appropriately guilty for it. But if he focused on his dick, he wouldn't have to think about other stuff, right? The thought of Mia had him immediately drifting. It was nearly mid-February, and she always showed up on the first of the month.

The ice was fairly thick on the mile stretch of water that separated them—what locals called The Break—but with all the freezing and re-thawing that had happened this winter, it was hard to tell if it was safe enough to cross. It was usually good by the first of January, but not always. If anyone else regularly crossed The Break, it would have been tested, every 50 paces or so, and a flag put up to mark the safe path. But it was only him on one side and Mia on the other.

He'd fantasized about loading up the 4x4 and taking the long way around to show up at the cabin across the way. Would she be surprised and glad to see him? It was the fear that she would be polite but reserved, welcoming but distant, that stopped him in his tracks. He knew the Mia who now lived her life across The Break and the Mia who came to him when the February ice was thick enough were two very distinct women.

He didn't move when he saw the flash of antlers out of the corner of his eye. He'd been doing this too long to make mistakes. The buck was an impossibly huge twelve point, pawing at the edge of the woods and lifting his head, sniffing for any sign of danger, in spite of the fact that two does and three fawns drank quietly from the stream.

Luke waited for him to move, looking through his telescopic lens and searching for the right angle. The sun was just coming up over the trees, casting a thick, orange shadow over the snow. His wait was going to pay off. He could feel it in the tightening of his belly, forgetting about the numbness in his left leg, the ache in his balls. Everything seemed to narrow down to this moment as the buck stepped into the clearing, lifting his head high. He only had one chance. This was the moment he lived for.

Luke took the shot, firing off several right after another, trying to make sure he got it. He was a football field away from them, but still, the deer heard the foreign sound of his camera's shutter and scattered across the field, their hooves kicking up thick clouds of snow in their wake. The buck ran back toward the trees and disappeared, leaving the clearing shuddering in the sudden stillness.

Groaning, Luke put his camera in its case, stretching out his aching legs. He hoped they would hold him on the walk home and that the film waiting to be developed would pay for the winter's cord of wood he'd ordered brought in. He'd found he didn't have the stamina to chop it himself anymore. *Not gonna need it if it doesn't get any damned colder.* It wasn't global warming that worried him really—like the fact that he'd seen more snowy owls than ever this year, due to the decreasing lemming populations further north. He would die long before the world solved that problem. It was Mia. Where was she?

He thought about her on the long walk home. If something had happened to Mia... *Not again, please, I can't stand one more grabber.* That's what his mother used to call those things that leapt out of nowhere and surprised the piss out of you—grabbers. He'd had enough of those to last a man a lifetime, and the thought of losing Mia made him feel like God had his balls in a vice. *You only really "have" her two weeks out of the year!* Maybe that was true, but he knew she was there, right across the lake, the rest of the time. Looking out at her cabin was both a comfort and a reminder.

In spite of the warmer weather, it was cold enough for his cheeks and nose to feel numb by the time he got back to the cabin. *Cabin, my ass.* Five years and what had started out as a lean-to had slowly grown into some semblance of a home. Luke shaded his eyes against the sun coming up across The Break. There was smoke wafting from the chimney of Mia's log home. She's all right, he told himself, kicking the snow off his boots on the porch steps. It's just not safe to cross. *Better safe than sorry.*

He put his camera bag on the table and unbuckled his boots, shedding his outer clothes. He left them hanging over the two chairs he'd made himself that matched the table sitting in the middle of what served as his living room, kitchen, and bedroom. His boots went near the woodstove to dry. The door next to the bed led to the bathroom—almost every time he used it, he remembered having to install the pump himself. *Never again.* Hazards of living in the middle of nowhere. He relieved himself with a low, satisfied groan. Having his cock in his hand reminded him of Mia—how hungry and desperate she often was when she showed up on his doorstep, the way she wanted to swallow him whole. *Where are you, Mia?*

A voice in his head whispered, *she's been lost to you for years.* Yeah, well. So it came down to being grateful for two weeks in February. He took what he could get. Luke washed his hands and retrieved his camera bag, anxious to develop the roll in the can. Aside from the bathroom, the dark room was the only other separate room in the cabin—and it was bigger.

A red haze filled the room when he flipped on the light and shut the door. He unzipped the padded Cordura field case, fishing out the camera. He readied everything and flipped out the light again. His fingers fumbled with the latch on the camera's side and he sighed, taking a deep breath and waiting. His limbs didn't always cooperate when he wanted them to.

Gonna just stop breathing one of these days. Yeah, well. Weren't they all? So he'd been diagnosed with a disease that most men didn't get until they were in their seventies. Life just liked to reach out and grab you like that, sometimes, it seemed. Shy-Dragers syndrome was probably going to take his life—but he kind of rather hoped it would be a tussle with a bear or a cougar that got him in the end. Probably just wishful thinking. His body would succumb to the Parkinson's-like symptoms over time. He didn't like to think about it much.

He got the latch on the second try and the camera back popped open. He had considered going digital—everything was done on computers now. He had a little laptop and a scanner. He even had access to the Internet, thanks to satellite technology, but he rarely sent his photos that way. He still used a medium format camera, developed his own pictures, and drove an hour to the post office to mail them in stiff envelopes marked: PHOTOS DO NOT BEND.

He pulled the film spool out of its slot and his uncooperative hands shook it right out of his grip. *I was out in the cold way too damned long today.* It made a tinny sound when it bounced on the wood floor and ricocheted under the darkroom developing table.

"Hell!" Luke flipped the red light on again and sank to his knees, peering into the darkness underneath. He could barely see anything—the soft red light didn't reach the far corners. *Could be anything under there.* Yeah. Life had a way of jumping out and grabbing you. He shoved his arm under, feeling along the floor. Lots of dust and spider webs, but no film. No monsters either. He sighed, resting his cheek against the floor. The flashlight was in the other room. He decided it was worth one more look—or rather, feel.

The film had rolled all the way to the wall. His fingers barely touched it as he grunted and attempted to shove his shoulder under the table. *There! Got it!* Something moved under his fingers as he slid the spool across the floor, and he pulled that out, too. He knew the feel—he would know it if he went blind—it was the paper he printed his photos on. A lost print. He smiled, pulling them both out, anticipating his discovery.

If he hadn't been on the floor already, he probably would have ended up there. "Oh hell..." *How old is he here? Two, three?* It wouldn't be written on the back, like most family photos: *Kit Summer 2000.* No, this picture had slipped away, one of a million prints, never missed—just sitting and gathering dust until this moment, until the image of his son was accidentally revealed to him again after all these years. *How old would he be now?* He didn't want to know. He didn't want to remember.

Kit's bright eyes smiled at him in the picture—and he did remember. "Look at meeeeeeeee, Daddeeee!" Balancing on one foot on a log with the grace of a gazelle, his arms out as if he could fly. *Oh Kit...* He could fly. He did fly. Luke's hand shook—but this was no symptom of some fatal syndrome—and his throat felt as if it were swelling. Standing slowly, his legs trembling, he put the picture and the film on the table. He was no longer eager to reveal the images he had captured.

* * * *

At first he thought it was a moose or a wayward caribou. *If Mia knew I had mistaken her for a moose...* The cabin door opened, letting in the cold air, and Luke breathed in her scent—no roaming herd animal—but the bright, fresh smell of night and of Mia, shaking off the chill and putting down her pack.

"Luke?"

He rolled toward her, pulling the down comforter with him, but didn't answer. He listened to her shrugging off her coat and unzipping her boots in the dark. The wood stove burned low, giving off a little light, but not much. He waited until she came to the bed, sitting on the edge, before he spoke.

"It's not safe to cross."

He felt more than saw her shrug. "I made it."

"Do you have a death wish?"

Mia stood, pulling off her shirt and dropping it to the floor. "Probably." Her jeans followed, and she slid under the covers beside him naked. "But it's colder at night—I thought the ice would be a little more frozen."

"And no one to save you if you fell through." His hands found her in the dark, touching someone else's flesh for the first time in a year. His fingers sank into the softness of her hip, pulling her belly to belly with him.

The silence stretched long and Luke felt the weight of it before she finally spoke. "You know as well as I do the current would take me before anyone could reach me."

He pulled her close, wanting to melt the sudden chill. Mia softened against him, letting him hold her. Her skin was cold and he rubbed her to warm it. "I missed you," he admitted. It was always this way, every time he touched her. The constant rat wheel in his head stopped spinning the minute she slid her slender fingers over his chest. "I don't want anything to happen to you."

"I'm okay." She touched her forehead to his. Her breath smelled sweet, like carrots.

"No you're not."

She smiled against his mouth. "I know." Their first kiss in a year—it was like starting kindling under a log, slow to catch at first, but growing brighter the more they fed it. Her lips were soft and warm, but trembling, and she stiffened when he slid his thigh between hers, rolling her on top of him in the darkness. He wanted to keep her—that was his desperate, secret wish, one that he didn't want her to know and tried not to convey in the way he advanced.

Luke had long years of practice in approaching a wounded animal. Mia wasn't feral, like most. She was a trapped bird, heart beating fast, wings flittering, hard to keep still long enough to free her. Something in her was always struggling, and he longed to calm her. His strokes were long and light, top to bottom, his hands moving down and over her behind. He sought the hair-tie she used to keep it back, freeing the dark length and letting it spill over him in a silky cascade. It tickled his nose but he didn't move as she softly pressed her mouth to his.

It was just a matter of timing. He let her go and she sat up and straddled him, her fingers tracing over his collarbone, down his arms, along his sides, pressing his belly hard as if testing him for solidity, finding his edges and boundaries. The soft clutch of her thighs against his hips and the radiant heat of her sex shifting against his lower belly made him long to grab and take her. *It's been too long.* Still, he waited, listening for the change in her breath as she rocked against him, shifting her body lower with every wave.

"Luke...?"

She had found him, rising up hard against her bottom, and her fingers fluttered there, hesitant. *And I thought guys in my condition couldn't get it up anymore!* He'd had a brief moment of worry, considering the doctor's recent diagnosis—but Mia was Mia. His body responded to her, Pavlovian, nerve pathways seemingly dead for ages lighting up in quicksilver sequence at her touch.

"Hm?"

Her hand gripped him as she slithered down between his thighs and rested her cheek along his length, pressing cock to belly for a moment, breathing in deeply. "I'm leaving tomorrow."

His hand found her hair, stroking. "I know."

One night, two weeks—what did it matter? Mia was Mia. She nuzzled him, catlike, rubbing her hair and cheeks against his cock and belly, her hands gripping his thighs as she took the head into her mouth. *Oh god.* Her reserve broke like an avalanche, threatening to bury them both in the flood, and he tried to outrace it, stay just ahead of it, but there was nowhere to run. Mia unleashed was a force of nature, her moans like the crying of the wind as she took him deep into her throat.

She sucked his cock as if it were her salvation, and Luke sometimes thought that it might be—this last, tenuous human connection, their flesh coming together again after so long apart. He belonged to her in those moments, and she devoured him, unmindful even of his response, the inevitable thrust and growl and gasp of him. She was taking and giving all at once, as if she could draw life and breathe it back into him along the swelling length of his cock. Her saliva made a wet pool at the base, her hunger still clearly unsated as she gulped down his length. He groaned, feeling his control beginning to slip. It wouldn't be long, if she kept this up. *And here I thought I might at least get a little more endurance out of this damned disease!*

He considered grabbing her hair and pulling her off, but his experience taming the untamable told him it would be a mistake. Her fervor was going to slow—he could sense it in the hitching of her breath, the almost imperceptible slowing of her hand. His cock throbbed under her tongue and he took a deep, shaky breath, trying to curb the inevitable. It was no use. She was either going to stop, or he was going to come, but he wouldn't force her.

Her moans were like wails, the sound competing with her hand and mouth slicking up and down his length, and he had a moment to wonder if half of the wetness between his thighs might be tears. He got his answer when she stopped suddenly, sobbing as she pressed her forehead to his thigh. It was a desperate sound, and he wanted to reach for her, comfort her, but he knew better.

He waited. Mia shifted her weight, rolling beside him onto her back. Both of them were breathless, trembling.

"I hate you."

Luke nodded in the darkness. "I know."

"Damnit!" She sobbed, shoving him in the side with her hip. "I don't want to I love you anymore!"

"I know." He closed his eyes and sighed.

Mia reached for him and he felt something tight in his chest finally loosen, like he could breathe again after being under water for long time. She pressed her trembling lips to his and he tasted her tears. "I just... want... the pain... to stop."

"I know."

Her fingers found him, hard still and slippery from her zeal. "Luke, please..."

"I know." He rolled onto her, making her take his weight, and she gasped, clutching at him. His mouth slanted across hers, taking what it wanted, and she gave it with tears still coursing down her temples and soaking the pillow beneath her head. Her arms went around him like she was drowning and he kissed her tears—licked them from her hairline, rubbed his grizzled cheek against her wet one. All the while, he rocked his hips into hers, grazing her slit with his thick length. She was wet there, too, weeping from every orifice, and he wanted it all.

"No, no, no!" Mia grabbed him as he slipped down between her thighs, fisting his hair and trying to pull him back to her. He knew what she wanted—but he knew, too, what she needed. His mouth found her, covered her, and he sank into giving her what he could. She still protested, her cries soft and growing softer, her breath coming faster as he spread her with his fingers and tasted her. The soft down covering her labia rhythmically brushed his cheeks as he swallowed her juices, pushing his way through the pink folds of her flesh with his stiffened tongue.

His hands pressed her thighs wide, feeling the taut stretch of the muscles there, working as she rolled her hips on the bed. She let him, now, wanting it, grinding toward it, and that made his cock twitch with a ferocious lust. He wanted to sink into the flesh where his fingers concentrated on their work, in and out of that tight, slick passage. Her fingernails raked his scalp as she began to quiver and rock. He'd sent her over the edge enough times to recognize it and he grabbed her ass in his hands as she pumped up toward his mouth with her climax, as if he could squeeze every last bit of pleasure from her body.

Ragged breathing and soft gasps had replaced her sobs and she reached down, asking for him. His cock ached, but he was still in no hurry as he kissed his way up over her swollen mound. He felt the long scar just along the top line of her pubic hair with his tongue and traced it, back and forth, until she growled and dug her nails into his arms, begging him. He covered her body with his and she sucked at his tongue, swallowing the taste of herself, biting at his lips.

"Ahhh god..." Luke moaned when she reached between them and squeezed his cock, stroking the length in her hand, right against her wetness. "Mia..." The sensation was exquisite and he let her for a moment, relishing the soft tug of her hand, the fleeting promise of her pussy as she rubbed him up and down her slit. When his lips found her nipple, she gasped, squeezing him harder and aiming him. He nudged forward, his hips pressing, feeling her flesh give a little.

"Oh yes!" She rocked her hips to meet him and his mouth left her nipple, slipping up to capture her mouth. He stayed poised there above her as they kissed, his tongue moving slowly in and out between her soft, open lips. The feel of her stretched beneath him, aching, longing, was almost enough. He felt like he could stay this way forever.

She broke their kiss, gasping. "Please... oh please, don't tease me." She kissed his stubbled cheek, wrapping her arms around his neck and whispering into his ear. "Fuck me, Luke. Fuck me so hard I won't remember anything again—ever."

He gave a soft groan, driving forward into her flesh, making them both gasp at the sensation. She was like velvet heat, gripping him, pulling him back in even as he withdrew, the outstroke almost as good as the first one in. His cock wanted more and he teased both of them with long thrusts, kissing her between each one.

Finally, nuzzling her ear, he whispered there, "Hard, Mia?" She nodded, giving just a whimper, pulling him down onto her, his full weight. He wanted what she did—to fuck until there was nothing left, until the world was spent and they were clear of it. She moaned when he began, a soft cry of anticipation, wrapping her legs around his waist.

His slow, easy strokes turned into a short, hard pounding as he sought to bury his cock into her deepest recesses. Mia cried out, biting his shoulder, but she met him, shoving her hips up for more until he thought he must be bruising them both. But neither of them cared—their flesh met again and again, saliva and sweat mingling as their tongues entwined, wetness spreading on the mattress beneath them. The rapid slap of their coupling filled the room, and his balls ached as they rocked against her ass, drawing up tight as he felt himself nearing some final relief.

"Harder!" Mia wiggled beneath him, her breath hot against his ear. "Fuck, Luke! Hard! Hard!" Her words made his cock twitch and he growled, gritting his teeth and propping himself above her for more leverage. *If I fuck her any harder...* But she wanted more, she begged for more, wild with it, scratching his shoulders, biting and sucking at his forearm, writhing beneath him like something caught, trapped, longing for freedom.

He gave her what she wanted, driving into her with an aggressive force that surprised them both. Using all of his weight, he drove himself deep, taking more and more with every thrust, gaining ground, driving her back on the bed until she pressed her hands above her head to keep from hitting the wall. And still, she pleaded...

"Don't stop!" Her breath came in short, ragged spurts. "Hard, baby, please, do it haaaaaarrrd!" The last word wailed from her throat and he felt the first thick spasm of her pussy, gripping him with a fleshy clench that was impossible to resist. Luke arched, letting out a low groan as he came, erupting into her soft, yielding flesh. The more he pushed, the deeper she seemed to go, taking more of him, until they were both spent, floating somewhere above it all together.

This is it. Deliverance... oblivion... absolution. It was all and none of those, and Luke's tears burned and he blinked them back, kissing her softly before rolling off. He wanted to say something, but he didn't know what. Instead, he pulled her out of the wet spot, spooning her against him under the down comforter and tucking it under her chin. She sighed, settling back, and it wasn't long before her breath told him that she was asleep.

"Mia." He whispered her name and kissed the top of her head. She would be gone again tomorrow, and although the thought twisted in his gut, he shoved it aside. He didn't want to remember anything, feel anything. He didn't want to be anywhere else but here, in this moment, listening to the sound of her breath fill the cabin and the screech of a snowy owl on the hunt outside in the light of a full moon.

* * * *

When Luke came out of the bathroom, she was gone. He was sure of it until he saw her pack by the door, her boots under the table. Pausing in the middle of the room with a towel wrapped around his waist, he surveyed it again. The sun had come up hours ago, and the light coming from the tiny windows in the front of the cabin was more than enough to show that the rumpled covers were kicked to the end of the bed, not hiding her sleeping form there. *So where—?* Her clothes were gone from beside the bed. He glanced again at her boots under the table. She wasn't outside. There was only one other place she could be.

That's when he heard her. Luke grabbed a pair of jeans, pulling them on as quickly as he could. His fingers didn't want to work in the morning and he fumbled with the snap, finally leaving it undone as her sobs grew louder. He had never installed the standard red caution light outside of his darkroom door—there was never anyone else to walk in to disturb him.

"Mia?" The red haze spilled out of the little room and he saw her curled into a corner, clutching the photo in her hand. "Oh fuck. Mia…"

"He ran ahead of me." The picture trembled in her fingers and he glimpsed his son's dark, laughing eyes. "He saw a deer…"

"You don't have to." Luke squatted beside her, reaching for the photo.

She clutched it to her chest, her eyes flashing, accusing. "Why didn't you stop me?"

His jaw clenched and he rested his head in his hands, staring at the floor. What was the right answer? What was the real answer? When did all of the rationalizations he told himself alone in the dark become reality? *What if, what if...*

He shook his head at her, meeting her eyes. "Why did you go?" She covered her face with the photo, sobbing. *Fuck. Why do we do this?* "It doesn't matter, Mia. It's... it just doesn't matter."

"It's not over." Kit's smiling face appeared, smeared with his mother's tears, his arms out as if he could fly. *Fly, little bird, fly.* "It'll never be over. I can't get it out. I can't—"

He pulled her to him and she fought, clenching the picture into her fisted hand and hitting him in the chest. Luke grabbed her wrists, twisting her arms in front of her and pulling her between his thighs as he sat with his back against the wall. He was at least still strong enough to hold her. He rocked as she struggled and cried, leaning his head back, his own tears leaking slowly and silently into his ears as he waited her out.

Finally exhausted, she let herself rest back against him and he loosened his grip, kissing the top of her head. "Don't leave, Mia."

"Don't leave? Oh Luke..." She shook her head and let out a short, strangled laugh. "What else can I do?"

"Stay."

"No." She jerked herself out of his grip, standing and steadying herself against the darkroom table and dropping the crumpled picture of Kit onto the floor. "I can't. Not today. I have to go." He let her, following her out and watching her pull her boots on. He tugged a sweatshirt on, sitting on the edge of the unmade bed as she put her pack up on the table and unzipped it.

"I didn't stop you because I was angry." Luke cleared his throat and Mia blinked over at him. "I told you it wasn't safe—you went anyway."

Her throat worked, her mouth opening, but no words came. She sank down into one of the kitchen chairs, her voice barely above a whisper, "I thought you were just saying that... because you wanted to stay..."

He'd tried to block too much of it to remember clearly, and he wondered if she had, too. They looked at each other across a space of four feet that suddenly felt bigger than the continental divide. Hanging his head and closing his eyes, he saw them both going, hand in hand. Kit was wearing his red hat and mittens, glancing over his stocky little shoulder once to look back. Luke remembered lifting a hand to wave, even as angry as he had been.

"You promised we'd sleep in the new cabin on his birthday." Mia dug through her pack, her voice shaking. "We promised him, Luke—and all you wanted to do was stay and chop wood!"

"I know." He didn't look up at her, remembering. It didn't matter anymore who was right, who was wrong. Ever impatient Mia, wanting what she wanted, when she wanted it—he told her to wait, that he would be done splitting wood in just a few hours for the lean-to they had been living in until the new cabin across the lake was completed. Then he could test the ice to be sure it was safe. He remembered the downturn of her mouth, the flash of her eyes. He remembered her returning, white-faced and trembling, clutching one red mitten in her fist.

"Here." She slapped something down onto the table, zipping her pack up and pulling on her coat. "Happy Birthday, Kit." The door opened, letting in the day's cold and brightness, and then she was gone. He thought about going after her—but what could he offer her now? He was dying—slowly, but surely. There was nothing left to give her but more pain. Luke sat for a moment, listening to her boots crunching on the snow, and then went to look at what she had left.

"Oh, Mia..." She had always been a writer. *You take the pictures, and I'll write the articles, and we can live out in the middle of nowhere together forever and be happy, just like you always talk about.* What did the girl ever see in him? Ten years younger, bright, beautiful—but she loved him, she inspired him. They had done it. Here they were, living together out in the middle of nowhere, taking pictures and writing, just like they had talked about. *Except...*

The book's cover was a white expanse of ice, and on it a woman bundled up, holding the red-mittened hand of a young child, a cabin in the distance on the other side. It was a thin book—a novel? He glanced under the title: *The Break—A Memoir.* He flipped through it and saw a bookstore bookmark stuck into one of the pages. She had highlighted a section in shocking, fluorescent pink and he sank into one of the chairs, reading:

I could never tell him what happened. I never could find the words to tell him how I killed our child. I blamed him, he blamed me, we blamed ourselves, and we swallowed that bitterness for months after Kit was gone. We swallowed it like medicine we were supposed to take every day, until the gap between us grew unbridgeable, and instead of sleeping in separate beds, we were sleeping in separate homes across the river that had taken our joy.

He knew, of course, what happened—but I never told him. I couldn't speak the words. The horror of that moment was something I carried alone until now. My heart slipped under the ice that day and drifted away, frozen and alone.

Kit ran ahead. That's all. I was doing what Luke had taught me—carrying a pickaxe and pounding it into the ice every 50 paces or so, making sure it was safe. But Kit saw a deer at the water's edge, and his little hand slipped out of his mitten and he was gone, running and calling after me to hurry. Hurry, hurry, Mama!

I wasn't fast enough. By the time I reached the place where he had fallen through, I could see him, but I couldn't reach him. The current was strong and it had pulled his little four-year-old body under so swiftly that, if I hadn't seen him go under, I might not have known he had been there at all. There was nothing to grab onto—he was trapped beneath the ice, and I couldn't do anything to get to him.

When I remembered the pickaxe, I swung it over and over in a hundred places, trying to chip my way to him, somehow break a hole in the ice. I wasn't strong enough—or the ice was, suddenly, too impossibly thick. I tried to keep up, whispering his name, and I remember saying, "No, no, no, no!" over and over as I followed him downstream.

I clearly remember the moment when his eyes closed. I don't know how long he was conscious—could he see me? What was he thinking? Hurry, hurry, Mama! I knelt there in the cold, sobbing, beating my fists on the snow-covered ice. His little red hat had come off, but he was still wearing the other mitten, its twin clutched in my hand. He looked almost like he was sleeping—his mouth open, eyes closed, head turned to the side. I watched my heart freeze and die and sink into oblivion...

Luke put the book down onto the table and grabbed his boots, buckling them as quickly as he could before pulling on his coat. When he opened the door, he could still see her, just a few yards into her trip back across. *What are you doing?* She had watched her son die, and if he went after her, would there be nothing left but to watch her husband die, too? Is that what he wanted to give her? *I don't want to love you anymore.* But she did. And he did. And until either of them finally flew, and drifted through this world and into the next, it was one thing they could both grab onto. He shut the door behind him and started on his way across The Break.

Author's Note:

No one knows what the effects of global warming may be long term—in fact, arguments continue to rage whether or not it actually exists.

Paved Paradise

```
Nicholas    Brody,   actor
best  known   for   his  role
as  Rick  on  the  hit  series
"Another  Saturday  Night,"
died   in   his   California
home  late  Friday.  It  was
an apparent suicide.
```

I would never forget the time Nick hung by one hand off the edge of a railroad trestle with a hundred feet stretching between him and the water below, just to write "Nick 'hearts' Jen" in white spray paint on the side. It was nearing the end of the summer, the best summer of my life, and he and I had been having a farewell picnic by the water when he produced a can of spray paint and told me what he was going to do. I couldn't stop him.

"This is our spot, Jenny," he told me, his eyes bright, with excitement or with love, I didn't know which, but it didn't really matter. I knew my protests would only plant the idea more deeply for him.

Besides, it was kind of romantic.

I watched him walk out to the middle of the trestle and then swing himself down. I had called a breathless and belated, "Be careful!" He had just grinned at me.

Thinking about it now, the blood slides through my veins like cold needles, but then it was kind of exciting. So much like Nick. When I look back and try to imagine my grandson, Eric, who was the same age now as we were then, pulling a stunt like that, all of my inner-warning-systems go off at once. I still can't believe I simply let him do it, without saying anything more than, "Be careful."

He could have killed himself.

* * * *

"Hey, why don't you look where I'm going?" Those were the first words Nick ever spoke to me. I had been on my way out of the back room where I had just finished putting my uniform on. (I refused to walk down the street in it.) That summer I was working in the soda shop in town. I had just turned eighteen in May and my mother finally agreed to it. I don't remember what I did with the money, spent it on clothes and such, no doubt, but money wasn't the real object anyway. Boys were.

He was a senior like us that year, tall and muscular and blonde. He was absolutely perfect, and I had put him on my list of "Goals for the Summer." Also on that list was: Get a Job, Lose Five Pounds, and Read Some Classic Novels. I accomplished every single one of them, including reading *Catcher in the Rye*. I read aloud to Nick when we were down by the lake. It was both romantic and practical. Perfect. Everything was perfect that summer.

I'd like to say that I came off with some witty reply. Patty would have. Instead, I mumbled, "I'm sorry," and stepped around him. He tugged on my dark blonde ponytail as I went by, and when I turned to look at him, he winked.

I was in heaven for the rest of the week.

He asked me to go to the movies with him the following Saturday.

* * * *

Our best times were down by the lake. He and I would take a picnic lunch and drive the Chevy past town and up a dirt road that had no name. Today, there's a K-Mart on that spot, and there is no road at all, but back in

1957 that road came to a dead end at the beginning of the woods. We would park the car and walk the rest of the way. Nick would spread out a blanket that he kept in the trunk of his car and I would unpack the lunch.

We would lay back on the quilt after lunch and he would put his head on my stomach. I would look up into the web of tree branches above my head, watching birds pop from tree to tree, listening to the rush of the water and Nick's voice.

"Jenny?"

"Hm?" I loved to stroke his hair, so soft and thick.

"Do you ever wish you could fly?"

"Fly?" I smiled at the notion.

"Yeah, you know, just put your arms out and then... whoosh... just take off. Never come back."

"Never?"

"Never," he whispered.

"Wouldn't you be scared?" I asked.

"No." He would rub his cheek against my stomach. "I'd be free."

I knew if anyone had heard us, they probably would have smiled or laughed. It sounded like inane conversation to me now, but I remember taking every word I said to him very seriously, as if it were the last time I would ever say anything to anyone again.

He scared me when he talked like that.

* * * *

My parents hated Nick. Maybe that was the reason I was so attracted to him. My father had been trying to push me all year into dating his boss' son, Raymond. Ray was a nice guy and all, very responsible and respectful—and boring. We went out a few times, but I didn't feel quite the same about him as I did about Nick. I could go weeks on end without thinking about Ray at all—but I couldn't get enough of Nick.

Patty was dating Greg Renke that summer. He was a junior, but he had a car, so it was okay. Nick had a Chevy Bel-Air that he liked to drive at sixty miles an hour (as soon as my house was out of sight!) Nick was the most excitement I'd had in my life up until that point. He was wild, reckless, and so awfully good-looking. I never understood why he chose me.

Parking got to be quite a challenge with Nick. Patty and I would both call and tell each other everything about what happened on our dates, but it got to the point where I was embarrassed to tell her exactly "how far" I had gone with Nick. He was persistent and very persuasive. It went further and further every time we went out, especially when we went to the drive-in. Patty and I shared a joke that it was something in the air at the drive-in, the smell of popcorn or something that turned men into animals.

It never went so far as intercourse. Good girls just didn't do that back then. But there were many, many nights that summer that we steamed up the windows, and I would eventually have to break things off, saying "I mean it this time!" Then Nick would get out of the car, walk around, adjust himself, talking to the sky. And I would sit there, fixing my hair and lipstick in the rear view mirror, watching him with a dull ache between my legs. I wanted to be a good girl, but I wanted to be Nick's girl.

* * * *

I never really understood what that feeling was until one night when things went further than they had ever gone before. We were stretched out side-by-side on the front seat, the drive-in movie not even halfway through the first feature. I never got popcorn or soda anymore, because I knew I never had time to eat it before we were pressed together like this, kissing and touching each other.

Nick had my bra undone, and his hand was under my blouse, kneading and fondling my breast as he kissed me. He was the best kisser, his tongue gliding like the softest velvet over mine. I got so lost in his kisses that before I knew it, my clothes were undone in places I hadn't even felt his hands.

"Nick, wait," I panted. Pantyhose wouldn't be introduced for another two more years, and my pleated skirt was riding far up past the tops of my stockings where my garters were holding them up. He had my skirt almost to my waist, and I pulled at it, but it was trapped between our bodies.

"Jenny, please," he whispered against my cheek. He had my nipple between his finger and thumb and he was rolling it back and forth. It made me feel funny between my legs. "Not yet."

I heard his acknowledgment that we had to stop... just not yet. I sighed, relaxing a little and letting him lift my sweater, exposing my breasts. I gasped when his mouth fell over my nipple. The first time I had felt his tongue there, I thought I was going to faint. I still wasn't used to the sensation, and it made me feel crazy and wild. I whimpered, trying to keep my hips still—they wanted to grind against him.

I heard him unzipping his pants and I held my breath. He wanted me to touch it, and had been trying to get me to for a week. Every time my hand reached the fleshy, pulsing thing between his legs, I drew back in terror. Tonight was no exception. He led my hand down there, using my fingertips this time to stroke the soft, meaty tip. It was a little wet, and I started to draw back. Was that pee? I made a face.

"It's ok." His voice was hoarse. "Please, Jen. It feels so good when you do it."

I reached my timid hand back between his legs, just grazing it with my fingernails. He shuddered. His hand was edging its way up my stocking. I could feel it resting on the bare skin of my thigh between the top of my stocking and the elastic edge of my panties as he kissed my breast. His tongue, flicking my nipple, sent electric jolts through my body.

"Doesn't it feel good?" he asked, edging his hand up a little higher. I squeezed my thighs together, not wanting him to go any further. I could feel wetness there, and was embarrassed by it. Still, his hand was nestled sideways between my legs, rocking upward. "Let me touch you. I just want to touch you."

His tongue moved over my nipple again and I sighed, closing my eyes. The sensation was heavenly, and the pressure of his hand rubbing up between my legs only increased it. He wiggled his hand back and forth, and he was moving right over that sweet, secret spot that felt so good to touch when I washed myself in the bath.

"Nick," I warned him, trying to wiggle away, but I was all the way back against the seat. The vinyl sighed and groaned as he pressed harder against me, shifting his weight so his hard, exposed flesh brushed up against my hand again.

"Doesn't it feel good?" he asked again, moving his hand faster. I tried to clamp down harder, to keep him from doing it, but it was no use. He moved his mouth to my other breast now, his tongue rolling around my nipple in circles. I gasped, turning to give him better access, in spite of the warning bells going off somewhere in my head.

My thighs relaxed their grip on his hand, and he slid his palm flat against my panties, rubbing me there. I moaned now, grasping the hard shaft between his legs and squeezing. He hissed against my breast.

"Oh, God!" he cried. "Jenny!"

I let go immediately, scared. "Did I hurt you?"

"No," he breathed, reaching for my hand and putting it back on him, wrapping my hand around it. "It felt good."

"Oh." I let him guide my hand up and down the stiffness between his legs, but I was afraid to look down at it.

His breath was coming faster as he used my hand, up and down.

"Nick," I murmur, watching his face, twisted in pleasure or pain, I couldn't tell. "Nick, stop."

He sighed, slowing, stopping. His eyes met mine in the dark. "What are you afraid of?"

I shrugged, blushing. "I don't know. I—I'm afraid of doing it wrong."

He smiled. "Would it be better if I show you how?"

I looked at him, my eyes wide. I couldn't imagine what he wanted to show me. "What do you mean?"

He sat up and leaned against the driver's side door, his hard flesh exposed, poking up through his zipper. I looked away, backing toward the passenger's side, aware of how exposed I was, too.

"Don't cover up, Jen," he said, his hand moving slowly up and down his rigid shaft. "Please."

I left my sweater pulled up over my breasts, my skirt cinched up to my waist. My knees were open as I watched him, fascinated, his thumb rubbing over the tip before sliding his hand back down the length.

"Does it feel good?" I asked, feeling a tingling in my breasts, between my legs. He nodded, his eyes shifting from one breast to the other, licking his lips.

"Doesn't it feel good when you do it?" he asked.

I blushed. "Do what?"

"Touch yourself," he said. "I want to watch you do it."

"I don't—" my face felt like it was on fire, and so did the mound between my legs.

"Pull down your panties, Jen," he said, his eyes on mine. "Please. I just want to see you."

I hesitated, watching his hand move over himself, up and down, a steady rhythm. I hooked my thumbs in the waistband of my panties and pulled them down with a little sigh of relief to be free of them. They were tight, girdle-like things, attached to my stockings with garters, and those came off, too, as I shed my panties. I left them bunched up at my feet.

"Open your legs," he said, his hand moving a little faster. I pulled my knees up, spreading them open. He groaned, looking at the dark patch between my legs. His hand was moving like lightning now, and I watched, fascinated.

"Oh, god, Jen," he whispered, his eyes half-closed. He stopped stroking himself, squeezing it so hard the tip looked purple in the dimness.

"Are you ok?" I asked. He nodded, and I heard him swallow.

"Would you—" he licked his lips again, his eyes falling to the triangle between my legs. "Would you spread it open?"

I gasped, blushing. "Nick!"

"Oh, please, Jen," he pleaded. "I won't touch you, I swear it. I just want to see... inside."

I reached tentative fingers down there. It wasn't like I hadn't touched myself before, washing in the bath, or wiping myself. Sometimes, I would even wake up from a dream and find my hand pressed between my legs, rocking with some aching sensation. But I'd never done anything like this in front of someone else before.

My lips were swollen and full, and I could feel a sticky wetness against my fingers as parted them. I didn't know what he could see in the dark, the drive-in movie throwing light and dim patterns over the windshield, but he gasped and moaned, his hand moving faster now.

"Does that really feel good?" I asked him, my fingers spreading myself a little wider, my eyes glued to the motion between his legs.

"Yeah," he panted. "Really, really good."

I swallowed hard, glancing around as if someone might see us. "Sometimes... it feels good... when I touch myself here." I pressed my fingers against the bud of flesh at the top of my crevice, shivering. God, it felt so good I could barely stand it.

"Do it, then," Nick said, watching my fingers intently. "Touch it."

I started moving my fingers there, nudging that little tingle, wanting it to grow. I used just one finger, back and forth, right over the top. He watched me, his head cocked, his mouth open, his eyes curious and excited all at once.

I moaned a little, feeling that tingle beginning to spread, my whole pelvis wanting to rock with it. I closed my eyes, moving my finger faster, and a little faster still, my tongue creeping out to touch the corner of my mouth. I remembered his tongue on my nipple, how much that had furthered that feeling between my legs, and I let the fingers of my other hand creep upward to my breast, tweaking my own nipple.

Nick groaned out loud and I peeked out at him. His eyes were half-closed, but he was still watching me. His hand was moving so fast up and down the length now that it was just a blur. The motion reminded me of my mother's sewing machine.

"Oh, Jen," he moaned, his hips shifting forward. My breath was coming faster as I watched him, my fingers circling that spot now, feeling it moving, somehow, rising, reaching toward something. The ache between my legs was unbearable.

"Nick, it feels so good," I panted, squeezing my breast in my hand, rolling my nipple.

"I know," he whispered. "God, I never knew—"

I didn't know what he was going to say next, and I never found out. Something altogether wonderful and shocking happened to my body. I started to quiver, my thighs trembling, and then that tingle between my legs let go in delicious, pulsing waves. I gasped and moaned, my hips bucking, my head going back against the window.

"Oh, Jenny!" Nick thrust up hard, and I watched as he bucked and thrashed, too, thick, white fluid shooting from the tip of his flesh again and again, pooling on the vinyl seat in front of me.

I stared, open-mouthed, as his thing began to wilt. My ears were ringing, and my head felt too full. I glanced at the pool of white fluid on the seat and tugged the twist of stockings and panties and garters back out of the way, working on untangling everything.

"Jen?" Nick asked. He was tucking everything back in, zipping up. I didn't answer him as I pulled my panties up over my knees, slipping my feet back into my stockings.

"Jen?" He moved to come across the seat toward me and stopped before he slid through the pool of liquid between us. I lifted my hips, inching my panties back up, pulling down my skirt, my sweater.

"I have something," I told him, reaching for my purse. I snapped it open and pulled out a handkerchief, dropping it onto the seat beside me without looking at him.

Nick wiped up the mess, sitting there with the cloth in his hand for a moment. "Uh—"

"Throw it away," I said, reaching around and re-hooking my bra. "I don't know how I could explain it..."

Nick chuckled, tossing the handkerchief up onto the dashboard and reaching for me.

"Are you ok?" He put his arm around me and I rested my head against his shoulder. On the screen, Old Yeller was fighting with a bear. We'd seen this movie so many times this summer, I knew it by heart. I probably could have quoted the dialogue without the speaker turned up.

"Jenny, I really love you." It was the first time he had said it. I lifted my face to look at him, still flushed with what we had done.

I said the only thing I could think of to say, and it was true, "I love you, too."

* * * *

"I'm leaving, Jen." The sun was shining on the lake and we held hands as we walked.

"I know." My chest felt constricted. Nick was going to the University of Southern California on a scholarship. He had told me ages ago, at the beginning of the summer.

"Will you miss me?"

"Dumb question." I smiled, bumping him with my shoulder. He stopped and took hold of my upper arms.

"I mean it, Jennifer," he said, his eyes dark, darker than I had ever seen them. He was serious when he called me Jenny. He had to be downright *grave* to be calling me Jennifer.

"I'll miss you." I nodded, unable to look away from him.

"I love you, Jennifer." He pulled me to him. "I'll always love you." He held me so tight I almost couldn't breathe and he buried his face in my neck.

We clung together.

* * * *

"Hey, Grandma!" Eric peeked around the corner, his hair wet. He had obviously just stepped out of the shower. "Dan and I are heading over to Barrymore's. Are you making dinner?"

"Your grandfather called," I said. "He'll be late. Dinner isn't until eight."

"Typical," Eric muttered, turning and starting away.

I looked back down at the paper on the counter. It was our local, weekly paper, and because Nick had hailed from here, they made a big deal out of his death.

The words blurred and I shook my head, tossing the paper aside. I hadn't thought about Nick Brody in close to forty years. Even Patty and I didn't talk about him. She had her hands full taking care of her ailing husband, who was suffering from Parkinson's.

I was thankful that Raymond was still healthy—and working just as hard as he ever had, building his dead father's business, well past our retirement age. Since Catherine had passed, he was focusing his attentions on Eric in hopes he might take over the business some day.

Barrymore's, a local hangout for the kids where Eric was headed now, a place which included go-cart racing and a driving range, had been built right over the spot Nick and I used to go down by the lake. Ray had bid for and won the contract, literally paving over the paradise I'd once known.

So much life had happened between then and now. It was a million years ago that Nick and I had laid under the stars and talked about flying, the meaning of life, and the art of dying. A million years.

"Bye, Grandma." Eric leaned over to give me a perfunctory kiss on the cheek as he shrugged on his coat.

"Bye, honey." I must have sounded sad because he gave me a quizzical look.

"You okay?" he asked, looking at me with his dark green eyes, his mother's eyes. I smiled. Eric was so predictable, so stable, so much like his mother. She would have done a good job raising him, if she had lived.

"I'm fine." I smiled my best old lady smile. "Have a good time, and don't forget, dinner at eight. Your grandfather won't want to wait."

"He won't be here." Eric frowned. "He'll call at eight and say, 'Jennifer, I have to work a little later, could you—?'"

"Eric, please." I waved him toward the door. "Just be here. For my sake. If your grandfather does show up, he won't want to wait."

"Tell him not to." Eric made a face, heading toward the door.

"Be careful!" I called after him.

"I will," he replied. All the confidence of youth.

I went to the window and watched him pull out of the driveway. Then I just stood there, staring out and remembering things better left buried.

Author's Note:

Every single minute of every day, America loses two acres land.

Source: American Farmland Trust

Genesis

August 2020

    I knew my brother wasn't normal the minute he was born. Mama said, "Zoe's just jealous of the baby"—she told everybody that, but it wasn't true. I loved him like I loved the sun—big and bright, but really hard to look at right-on. It was like that, like he gave me sunspots whenever I stared at him too long.

    Not that there was anything wrong with him on the outside. Mama was quick to point that out, even after all the flapping started, the head-banging at night in his crib, the constant wailing, every day at the same time like clockwork, winding down at fifteen minute intervals and then starting up again until it went on for a whole hour.

    I was ten when I asked my papa what was really wrong with Jack. My brother was five by then, and Mama said he just wasn't ready yet to start in school. I didn't think Jack would ever be ready. I couldn't imagine him sitting at a desk like I did every day. He could focus on what he wanted, when he wanted… but if you tried to change his course, "Jack, look, how about we do it this way?" he would howl like you were tearing out his insides. He learned, but he wasn't very teachable.

    "Jack's autistic." Papa handed me a tomato. We were picking them off the tall vine behind the house.

    I pondered this for a minute, wanting to ask what the word meant, but too afraid to look like I didn't know.

    Papa smiled at the look on my face. "Remember when we took a trip out to the orchards last month?"

    I nodded. I loved going on bee-trips with Papa. He was known as the Bee-Man all over the country, and people would call just to ask his advice. Nearby farms and orchards knew how good Papa's bees were, and he rented them out to folks sometimes. "The right folks," he said. I didn't know what that meant, but I loved loading the hives up in the truck and taking them out to nearby orchards so they could pollinate the crops.

"Do you remember what you asked me?"

I nodded, saying the words just as I remembered them, "What's wrong with their bees?"

That was my question, riding high on my father's shoulders as he went up and down the orchard rows. He kept saying ten was too big to ride up high like that, but I was little for my age and insisted. Somehow he didn't seem to mind.

"Do you remember what I said?"

I tucked another tomato gently into the basket. "That something was wrong inside their bees. They were…broken."

Papa frowned, sighed, pinched off another stem. "But do you remember what else I said?"

"It wasn't the bees fault." I accepted another ripe fruit, my eyes drawn to the house, where Jack was standing on the wide front porch, spinning. He could do that for hours. Sometimes he did it until he threw up. But even then, he wouldn't stop, unless Mama made him—and then he'd scream up in his room, pound the door, kick the walls.

I shaded my eyes against the bright sun, looking up, way up, at my father. "But… whose fault is it, Papa?"

He put his big hand on top of my head. "It's our fault."

"Can we fix it?" I glanced at Jack, spinning, spinning.

"I don't know." Papa sighed, handing me another tomato. "I hope so."

August 2025

"Zoe, wake up!"

My eyes didn't want to open, and I knew it had to be either very, very late, or really, really early. Jack persisted, though, poking and nudging me awake by degrees until I finally hissed at him in the darkness.

"This better be good!"

"I want to show you something."

I threw the covers off in a huff, swinging my feet over to look at the clock. Three in the morning. Just great. Jack was wearing a goofy headlamp, and nearly blinded me when he looked in my direction.

"Shut that stupid thing off."

"We're going to need it."

I sighed, rubbing my eyes and reaching for the jeans I'd left at the end of my bed. I knew there was no sense arguing. He would just have a fit if I didn't go, and I wasn't about to initiate anything that might wake our parents at three in the morning, not the way Mama had been feeling.

It had started some time around my high school graduation in June. She wouldn't go to the doctor, although Papa kept saying he was going to take her, that scared look in his eyes. I didn't know if they were going to make it.

"Jack, get that thing out of my eyes!"

He tilted it up toward the ceiling, giving the room an eerie glow. I could see his face now, eyes bright and full of excitement. My brother didn't spin or flap or scream anymore, but there was still nothing really normal about him, and that showed especially in his eyes. To me they always looked as if he was counting something in his head, endless rows of numbers, as if he were a human calculator. But Mama was right about one thing—he had turned out to be brilliant, in his own peculiar way.

I slept in a t-shirt, so I just tucked that into my jeans and grabbed a flannel out of the closet. It was mid-August and still hot as hell outside, but there would be mosquitoes.

"Ready?"

I sighed again, trying to figure away out of this middle of the night adventure, but looking at Jack's face, I just couldn't think of one, so I followed him out into the hall and down the stairs. Our parents were sleeping—I glanced into their room as we passed—

Papa snoring like a buzz saw and our mother curled into a small, tight ball on the other side of the bed.

"Where are we going?" I whispered as we stepped out into the humid night. I looked up and saw at least a million stars. We were far out of the city, and there were no neighbors within half a mile in any direction. All of our land had belonged to Papa's family for over a century.

"The laboratory." Jack went, expecting me to follow, and I did. He called it the laboratory, and I suppose it was something of that sort. I think it was Papa's idea to give him the chemistry set, although the idea scared the bejeezus out of me and Mama, just like the year before, when Jack insisted on learning how to target shoot.

"I hate it down here." I shivered, although it wasn't cold. Jack ignored me, shutting the storm doors behind us and sliding the wooden bar down to lock us in. It was an old tornado shelter, but my brother had turned it into Jekyll and Hyde's workroom. There were test tubes and beakers and all sorts of tubing set up. He turned on the light—one hanging bulb with a looped chain that swung like a hangman's noose above our heads.

"Zoe, look."

I heard the buzzing before I saw them. He had bees down here! My jaw dropped and I looked at him with wide eyes. He shrugged one shoulder, knowing as well as I did that if Papa found his bees down here, he'd skin my brother alive and probably me along with him, just for knowing about it.

"What am I looking at?" I murmured, taking another step toward the hive. They were in one of Papa's organic top bar hives instead of the usual box. It was a more natural way for them to work, and Papa said they were much more productive that way.

"Those aren't Papa's bees," Jack told me, crossing his arms and waiting. His limbs were way too long for his body lately, all in the way. It was still hard for me to believe he was a teenager now.

"Okay." I shrugged, although I was unbelievably relieved. Papa's bees had become more and more valuable not just locally, or even nationally, but worldwide, as the bee shortage grew worse and worse. "So he won't kill you. Where did you get them?"

"Remember Ruby's Orchards?"

I frowned, taking another step toward the hive. They were buzzing busily, even though it was the middle of the night. I suppose a bee's work never ended.

"But their bees are all gone. They disappeared. That whole colony collapse disorder, or whatever it is…"

Ruby's had bought a few hives from Papa, but it wasn't long before they had disappeared. It wasn't unusual. The bees had been disappearing for years, and while no one knew the cause, Papa kept saying it was because they didn't know how to care for the bees naturally.

There was such a shortage of food in third-world countries now that Papa said we'd be starving in the good old US of A if we didn't do something about it and quick. The nightly news was full of crime, looters, people stealing other people's food. Human beings did strange and awful things when they were hungry. But we didn't feel it much, considering we had our own bees to pollinate what we grew in the garden.

"They're not gone anymore," Jack said proudly.

"You *resurrected* the bees?"

"Well...not the dead ones." He grinned. "But I did bring back the missing ones."

"You did not!" I took another step toward the busy hive. They certainly sounded healthy.

"I did too!" he insisted. "Everyone thinks they've been dying—but they haven't."

"What are you talking about?"

"They just go somewhere else. Somewhere they can...get better."

I stared at him, just blinking, but he went on like he didn't see the dumbfounded look on my face.

"It's not one thing, Zoe. It's not mites or genetically modified food or pesticides—it's everything. *Everything* around them becomes too much, too intense, and eventually, their whole environment makes them so different they can't stand it anymore."

His description reminded me so much of him, the way he was, that it was startling, and I wondered if he realized it. Then, when he turned to me, and I saw the look in his eyes, I knew he did. "They found a way out...or through...or..."

"Where?"

"Through the honeycomb."

I snorted. "Jack, this makes no sense..."

"Papa's always talking about honey and all its practically magical healing properties, right? I mean, according to the laws of physics, bees shouldn't even be able to fly. But they do."

I shrugged. It still didn't explain anything. I hugged myself and frowned. It was creepy down here, and I wanted to go back to bed.

"Did you ever wonder why honeycombs are so perfectly hexagonal?" Jack asked. "And the ends of each one is trihedral—it actually creates a pyramid. It's like...it's sacred geometry, Zoe. The bees don't fly away or disappear at all. They...they go through their hives to another place. A place where they can be whole again."

"Jack, I think you've gone crazy."

"I can show you." The set of his jaw made me wince. "I built one."

"One what?"

"A honeycomb. Big enough for me to go through. You, too, if you want."

I didn't say anything as I followed him back into the "laboratory." The light was dimmer here, but I could see what he'd been crafting well enough. He'd made it out of wax—just like the bees. I couldn't imagine how many hours it had taken to craft against the back wall of the cellar—and the entire structure covered the whole wall.

"What is it?" I whispered.

"I told you. A honeycomb."

"But there's no honey."

He snorted. "I'm not a bee. But I did find out where they go. Wanna see?"

Did I want to see? I watched as Jack slipped his head into one of the holes. It was just big enough for him to pass through, its perfectly hexagonal form accommodating his shoulders as he twisted further in.

"You're going to get stuck!"

"No I won't!" His voice sounded far away, blocked by his body, of course, but it seemed even further than that.

"Where are you going?" It seemed impossible for him to be disappearing into one of the waxy holes. How deep were they, I wondered, as his tennis shoe caught the edge and he kicked it free and slipped completely into the hexagon.

Then, impossibly, he was gone. I screamed—it happened before I could think about Mama sleeping upstairs, before I could think about anything at all—but it didn't matter, because no one up there heard me. The sounds upstairs were much louder than my little yelp of surprise and fear as Jack's head appeared again at the hole.

"Come on!" He insisted, frowning when he saw my face, and then heard the commotion upstairs. "What is that?"

"*Who* is that?" I whispered, looking up at the ceiling, hearing heavy footsteps, loud voices, none of them belonging to anyone I knew.

"Get in here!" Jack reached through and grabbed my shirt, pulling me forward so hard I hit my forehead on one of the waxy edges it would leave a bruise for a week. "Hurry!"

I let Jack lead me, my hands sliding on the waxy surface as I followed him into the hole he'd gone through.

That's when I heard a familiar voice: "You get the hell of my land, you goddamned Nazis!"

"Papa..." I whispered his name, but Jack was pulling me through into darkness.

"You can't take those! That's my private property!"

The voices were fading, and I could only feel Jack's hands, and a darkness that felt warm and sticky against my skin.

"Confiscate this!"

That couldn't have been a gunshot. It couldn't have been.

"What—?" I whispered.

Somewhere, Mama screamed.

The last thing I heard in our world was another shot, and then there weren't any more screams, just the sounds of big truck tires on the gravel drive, stealing away in the middle of the night, before my brother pulled me into the place where the bees came and went.

September 2030

"Two rabbits." Jack held them up by their feet, their dead eyes dull and staring like black marbles in their soft heads. "Sorry."

"It's enough for the two of us." I wiped my hands on my jeans—I never did get to wearing an apron like Mama had always done—leaving white streaks of what I was attempting to call "flour" there, although my experiment to make my own hadn't, so far, been too outrageously successful. "Can you skin them? I have to go check the hive."

My brother grabbed my arm as I headed toward the door he'd just come in. "Don't."

I raised my eyebrows at him. "I have to."

"There's someone out there, Zoe." He shook his head, insisting again. "Let me do it."

I rolled my eyes. "Jack, we've been alone in this cabin for five years. We haven't seen a single person since—" I stopped, not wanting to say it. I don't think the people who came for Papa's bees knew about the cabin, hidden back on the property under cover of the trees. Or if they had, they didn't care. No one had ever came looking for the two of us.

Of course, I had no idea how long we'd spent that night beyond the human honeycombs, trembling in fear and wondering what was happening to our parents, our world. Jack didn't know, either. Time was different there, and although he'd hinted about going back through again, I was too afraid. As strange and wonderful as the experience had been, we'd come out to find our own world, as we knew it, completely gone, and I had no interest in trying out any more of Jack's science experiments, thank you very much.

"If you're hearing something, it's probably a deer or a big coon."

"Fine." Jack didn't look like he believed my explanation any more than I did. "Take the gun."

"No." I made a face, slipping on my shoes. "I hate that thing. I'll be fine. Besides, we don't have any more bullets."

We'd run out of ammunition two years ago, but thanks to Jack and his ability to build things, we had all sorts of ingenious traps set up around the woods.

"He won't know that," Jack reminded me, his eyes pleading.

"He?" I snorted, shaking loose. "It's a 'he' now?"

"Just—"

"Nope." I shut the door behind me and bounded down the steps, glad for the fresh air and the walk down the path toward the hives. I'd been cooped up in the kitchen way too long, canning and trying to put up food for the winter, which wasn't easy when we had to shut off the generator every hour or so to conserve energy.

The windmill Papa had installed when we were little served to provide us with rudimentary power, and the generator, which ran on biodiesel that Jack made in enormous vats, supplemented the rest. Still, we had to be careful. Gone were the days of microwaves and electric can openers and televisions—but then, even when we'd had one of the latter, there hadn't been anything on it for three years. The rest of the world, it seemed, didn't have any power, either.

Not that I missed it. We'd always been isolated, tucked away into our own little corner of the world. I didn't miss cars or radios or computer, but I did miss people. I missed Papa. I missed Mama. I missed talking to someone beside my brother, whom I loved, but like any sibling, could be a pain in the butt. And Jack was usually so preoccupied with something, he wasn't much fun to be around anyway, unless you wanted to talk about solar panels or radiation. Just for once, I would have liked to tell a joke and have someone laugh instead of just look at me.

We kept the hives hidden, still, after all this time. Our parents had died for these bees, and Jack and I were more than protective of them, we were militant. The men who had come to take the Bee Man's bees hadn't known about these, the ones living out by our cabin in the woods. They might, I thought as I neared the hive, be the very last bees in the world for all I knew.

I found myself humming, just like Papa used to, whenever I worked with the bees. When I asked him once why he hummed, he looked surprised, like he didn't know he was doing it. "I guess it's my way of talking to them," he said. "Telling him I'm not here to hurt them, that it's going to be okay." I got that immediately—because he could do that for me in an instant after a nightmare with a hand on my forehead and a low, gentle hum buzzing deep into the night.

Somehow I'd learned through osmosis what he knew. My throat found the same resonance as the bees' song, just like his had, and I sang it as I worked, checking the hives for honey production, making sure the bees looked healthy and strong. I was glad I was done—or almost—when he stepped out from behind a tree. Bees don't take well to being startled, and we probably both would have been stung to death. Although, I've wondered since, if maybe that would have been better...

"I thought they were all dead?"

I jumped like someone had stung me, whirling to the sound of an unfamiliar voice. I hadn't seen another human being in so long, I stared like he was an alien, but he was just a normal man—tall, big, his hair long, to his shoulders, with a full, thick beard, he wore a tattered jean jacket and jeans with holes in the knees. When he stepped forward, I took a step back, but the bees were in the way.

"Who are you?" My voice was nowhere near as strong or steady as I wanted it to be as I sidestepped the hive and took another step toward the direction of the house, already lamenting not bringing the useless but threatening-looking gun.

"Question is, who are you?" He smiled, and I think he wanted it to be friendly-looking, but his mouth and eyes were too tight for that.

"I have to get home now." Years of living on my own, and I immediately reverted to some little girl when I was standing before a stranger.

"Home? Where would that be?"

I opened my mouth to tell him—I was actually going to say—when he closed the distance between us in two long strides, grabbing my arm and pressing my back hard against a tree.

"I haven't seen a woman in years." He said that, but he wasn't looking at me. Instead, he used his hips to grind his pelvis into mine, his face moving against my hair. He was big and heavy, and the tree bit at my back as he pressed a thigh up between my legs, making me gasp in shock and a sudden, dawning horror.

"Please," I started with a plea, and knew it was all wrong. I turned my head when he tried to kiss me, and his mouth landed on my cheek, moving to my neck, his beard thick and itchy as he grabbed my breasts in both hands and squeezed.

"Stop!" I insisted. "My father is coming and he has a gun!"

It was all I could think of to say, but it was no use. The man was lost in his own world, as if I weren't even there at all, already fumbling with the zipper on his jeans. I screamed when he shoved me down to the ground, scrambling to find my footing, but he was on me too fast, my dress up to my waist, spreading my legs and yanking my panties down to my knees.

I tried to keep my legs together, but that didn't work either. The weight of him was too much for me, and he forced them open, tearing my underwear—I lamented as the sharp, ripping sound filled the clearing. He went to rip the front of my dress, too, and I shouldn't have, but I stopped him and unbuttoned it. Damned if he was going to ruin any more of my clothes.

He took this for consent—even eagerness—burying his face between my breasts, pressing them together and sucking hard at my nipples. I whispered, "No," turning my reddened face away, but there was no one to hear. His thick length of flesh nudged between my legs, thrusting, looking for an opening, but I wasn't about to help him do that.

"Gotta get you wet," he murmured, and I didn't understand what he meant until he spit in his hand and rubbed it into my cleft, making me shudder beneath him in a strange mix of pleasure, pain and horror. "God, your pussy feels so good...I haven't felt a pussy in..."

His moan and my scream drowned out the rest of the words as he plunged deep into my body. Nothing could have prepared me for the sensation—I felt as if I were being torn in two, and yet his face was a study in pleasure, eyes half closed, back arched, lip drawn under his teeth.

"Ohhh fuck that's good!" He started moving—just when I thought it couldn't have gotten any worse—pinning my scratching, clawing hands at the wrists in his big grip, pressing them over my head, his face near my ear as he began to grind on me. His breath was foul, hot, and I turned away as he tried to kiss me again. Instead he pressed his mouth to my ear and whispered. "Oh baby, your pussy is so tight. Oh god that's good, you feel so good, you're sweet little pussy is gonna make me come so hard…"

In all this time I'd forgotten to scream, to cry out. I seemed to have forgotten how to make any noise at all. I was just waiting for it to be over, waiting for him to go away…but as I looked at the sheer bliss on his face, I had a sudden, horrific thought—why would he go away? Why would he go anywhere, after he finished? If it felt so good, why wouldn't he want to do it again? And again? And…

"No!" I struggled harder, although between his weight and grip, I knew I was going nowhere. "Stop! Stop it!"

"Ahhh fuck!" He gasped, shoving faster, harder. "Too late now, I'm gonna come!"

Did that mean it was over? He grunted and shoved and shuddered over me, the thing between my legs like a steel rod, piercing me to my very depths. After a moment, he sighed, collapsing, breathing hard in my ear.

"Get off me!" I gasped—he was heavy and I couldn't do much more than that. "Right now! Get off! Get *off*!" I floundered like I'd seen wounded fish do, pressed under the weight of Papa's heavy shoe.

"So good, so sweet," he whispered, kissing my neck, my ear, still breathing hard. "I'm think I'm gonna keep you until I wear you out…"

I screamed then, my worst fear realized, calling for Papa, Jack, someone, anyone, wasn't there anyone? The man above me grinned and arched, pressed his pelvis against mine, grinding some more, and I thought I would go insane. I couldn't do this again—never again.

"Gonna fuck you some more," he insisted, grabbing my wrists and I hit him with closed fists. He didn't really even seem to notice the blows.

"Jack!" I screamed, hoping he might hear me—the world was quieter than it used to be. "Help! Jack!"

"Shut up, cunt!" he growled, squeezing my wrists hard, pinning them over my head again. "Or I'm gonna give you just what you deser—"

I gasped as he collapsed on me, a different weight this time, a dead one. I struggled, panting with the effort to get him off me. His face was against my shoulder this time, and I heard a thick, choked sound coming from his throat, like he was trying to say something, but couldn't.

"Get off!" I found I could bring my knees up now, without his legs controlling mine, and used them as leverage, shoving him away and wiggling out from underneath. My dress was still up around my waist, my panties a ruin on the forest floor, my thighs covered in blood. The man didn't get up. He didn't come after me. He shuddered and gasped, his cheek against the dirt, his eyes wide, searching.

"Are you okay?" I actually asked him. I actually did. His eyes met mine for a minute, pleading, and then he was gone. His eyes didn't close, but he went out of them, just the same.

"Are *you* okay?"

"Jack!" The hand on my shoulder made me jump and I hugged him, already pulling my dress down and reddening with embarrassment at him seeing me like this. "Oh my god, Jack, he—"

"I know." He put his arms around me and I felt something long and cold pressed into my back. "I would have, sooner, but I had to load the dart gun…"

"The…what?" I stared as he brought it forward, showing me.

"I used bee venom," he explained. "Concentrated about a hundred times. I've been working on it a while, since we ran out of ammunition. It's not good to be without a weapon."

When I looked back at the man on the ground, this time I saw the small dart sticking out of the back of his neck, and finally understood.

"Thank you," I whispered, hugging him, tight. He hugged me back and I felt him swallow. His heart was beating almost as fast as mine. "It was…it was bad."

"I'm sorry." His voice was choked and I winced, shaking my head.

"It doesn't matter." I insisted. "Let's go home."

Jack hesitated, frowning. "What are we going to do with him?"

"Leave him for the animals."

That's what I said, and I didn't look back. *It's over.* It was over. That's what I thought as I took my brother's hand and we walked slowly back to the house.

May 2031

I was sound asleep when I heard the scream. It was one, long sustained wail and it gave me shivers as I slipped out of bed and stumbled into the hallway. It was nearing dawn, and there was enough light to see Jack was already there with his dart gun, his eyes wide.

"It's a woman," he whispered.

"Sounds like." It was amazing that either of us recognized the sound of another human voice.

We crept toward the sound slowly, discovering a woman bleeding in the middle of Mama's living room carpet with a man leaning over her. Jack raised his dart gun but I shook my head, holding him off. The man wasn't threatening—he was obviously trying to help, pressing one of Mama's quilts to her midsection, although it was quickly darkening with blood.

"Is she okay?" I knew I would startle him and I did, the man's dark head jerking up, eyes wide. He looked as startled to see us as we did to see him.

"She's—" He shook his head, pulled the blanket away, and I immediately saw the problem. She had six inches of sharp metal stuck through her abdomen. The woman's eyes were closed now, as if the last scream she'd managed had been too much for her.

"Jack, get more blankets."

My brother moved quickly, and that made me move, too, stepping forward and kneeling beside the woman. "What happened?"

"She fell."

The woman's eyelids fluttered and she turned her head toward the man, choking out words. "I'm sorry, Ian."

"Shh!" He leaned over to kiss her forehead, and I tried not to see the pain on his face as he took the blankets Jack offered, covering the shivering woman, pressing them gently around her wound. He wasn't trying to ebb the bleeding anymore, and I could see why. She was going to die. There were no hospitals, no doctors. There was no where to go in an emergency. In another world, at another time, an ambulance could have come and taken her, maybe helped her. Maybe.

"Can you take it out?" the woman's voice was hoarse, her eyes still closed. "It hurts."

"Don't." Jack shook his head, speaking softly. "It will make things worse."

The man—Ian—nodded, his dark eyes glancing at me, taking in my nightgown and the way my hands rested on my protruding—and still growing—belly. I'd had plenty of time to think about the fact there were no doctors or hospitals left in our world.

"I'm Ian," he said, looking between me and Jack.

"Zoe." I met Jack's eyes as he moved to the couch. "That's my brother, Jack."

He nodded again, taking in this information as the woman's eyes opened and she whispered, "Water."

He looked at me and I nodded to Jack. "We have a well."

Jack brought a glass full back, handing it to Ian, who helped the woman lift her head to sip at it. It dribbled down her chin, pooling in the hollow of her throat, and he dabbed at it with the blanket before setting the glass aside and watching as she closed her eyes again.

"How long have you lived here?" Ian asked, not looking away from the woman's face.

"All our lives," Jack said from his perch on the arm of the couch.

Ian looked up then, startled. "I didn't think there were that many people left…"

The woman moaned, her back arching, and I saw more blood flowering the bedspread wrapped around the metal stuck through her middle.

"Shhhh, Susan, it's okay." Ian's hand brushed her forehead, the dark hair there wet with sweat. "You're going to be okay."

Her eyes opened long enough for her to whisper, "Liar," with a half-smile on her face before she faded again.

He *was* lying, of course. We were all sitting in our living room, making small talk and watching a woman die.

"Is she...your wife?" I ventured to ask.

"No." He blinked, looking like he was trying not to cry, and I looked away. "Just a...traveling companion. It's good to have company."

"Where are you going?" Jack asked.

"North. We heard they're rebuilding up there. Rumor has it they've got electricity back, maybe even television."

I stared at the useless blank screen of the one still sitting in our living room, the focal point where all our furniture had once pointed. It still pointed there, of course, but it was just a ghost, a memory.

"Ian!" The woman—Susan—reached a hand out, and he took it, squeezing.

"I'm here."

It was the last thing she did. We sat there, whispering back and forth, trading information, while we waited for her to die. It was terrible, but there was nothing we could do.

We knew very little, as isolated as we were, but Ian seemed to know a great deal about what was going on in the world. He'd been walking northeast toward New York for two months, and Susan had joined him about three weeks ago. He'd been pleasantly surprised that they'd made it to Pennsylvania all the way from New Mexico.

No one noticed when Susan stopped breathing. There was no sound, no indication. She just stopped at some point while we were talking, and when Ian went to check on her, pressing his fingers to the side of her neck, he frowned, then shook his head.

"I'm sorry," I whispered

"Now what?" Ian's question hung there, and I knew it wasn't meant for us, but I answered anyway.

"You can stay here," I volunteered, ignoring Jack's startled look. "At least until tomorrow."

"Thanks." When Ian smiled, the whole room seemed to brighten. "I'll want to…bury her…something."

"Of course." I pulled the blanket up over her as he stood, looking down at the dead woman in our living room and wondering just what was going to happen now.

May 2032

Ian didn't just stay the night—he stayed. Jack didn't like the upset in his routine at first, having another face at the breakfast table, someone else talking at dinner, and like all things with Jack and his autistic tendencies, it took a long, long time for him to get used to it. I think the baby was almost six months old before he really stopped protesting Ian's presence, and that was because he'd starting spending all day in the woods, working on something he wasn't ready to tell anyone about. Sometimes he spent whole nights out there, and I worried, but Ian told me not to, and I trusted Ian. I felt safer with Ian than I ever had with anyone, even my own Papa.

"Rachel will be awake any minute," I whispered, pushing Ian's wandering hand down from my breast to my belly. I had named her after my mother, and she looked like her too, the same big eyes and wide smile.

"Jack will entertain her," he insisted, his hand moving the other direction now, working itself between my thighs, making me sigh and rock against him. My education about sex and baby making had come a long way since that awful day in the woods.

"Jack didn't come home again last night," I murmured. I'd been up to nurse Rachel before dawn, and his bed hadn't been slept in.

"The mad scientist is up to something." Ian's fingers parted my lips, looking for heat and finding it. I couldn't help arching, pressing my behind against the swell of his hardening cock.

I hadn't told him yet, but since I started giving Rachel some of our mashed up food from the table, she'd been nursing less, and my period had returned. Well, once anyway. And now it was gone again, two months now, and the sickness in the morning that I'd had during my first pregnancy was enough to tell me what was happening to my body this time around. I wanted nothing more than to have Ian's baby inside of me.

He groaned when I reached around and grasped his length, squeezing, tugging, as his fingers worked between my thighs. I wanted him in me, always, to keep him with me. We never talked about what had developed between us, how it had come about, where it was going. It was a daily miracle to me, waking to find him in my bed, in my life, buried deep between my legs again and again.

"So hard," I murmured, rubbing my thumb over the tip the way he'd taught me. Turning in his arms, I slid down to take him into my mouth, another thing he'd taught me well, and his hand, still sticky with my juices, went to my hair, guiding me.

"Oh god, Zoe, yeah…" He thrust gently and my hand crept down so I could touch myself, my fingers seeking depth, mimicking the motion, aching to be filled. I loved pleasing him, hearing his moans as I flicked my tongue along the ridge before taking as much of him again as I possibly could. I wanted to stay here forever, sucking and licking and listening to his pleasure, but I heard the baby awake, playing in the crib Ian had made for her, and knew it wouldn't be long before she was insisting on breakfast.

"Your turn," I whispered, moving up over the hard planes of his belly and chest, letting him grab me with his thickly muscled arms, steady me with calloused hands as his mouth found my core. "Ohhhh Ian... oh yes, yes... lick it... ohhhh..."

Sometimes I thought my pleasure pleased him more than his own. He was always greedy for me, his tongue lapping, his mouth sucking at my flesh, and the way his hands cupped my behind, pulling me toward him, made it impossible not to thrash against him, begging for release. The baby cooed and laughed in the other room and I pressed my hands to my lower belly, knowing we would have another next year and he had given this—all of this—to me.

"Ian! Oh! Oh, now!"

He kept on, tenacious, drawing my orgasm out of me like he had everything else—with a gentle persistence I simply couldn't resist. I had given him everything, had birthed my baby into his hands, had come to his bed as if he were a magnet, and now I didn't hold back anymore. I shuddered and shook as I bucked my hips against his eager, delicious tongue, letting him take all of me. He groaned as he felt me quiver, his fingers digging deep into my flesh, and I knew if I glanced behind me, I'd see his cock weeping with excitement.

He wanted me as much as I wanted him, and although it was beyond my comprehension, I was grateful for it. I'd barely had enough time to recover, my head bent, hair in my face, panting and resting my hot cheek against the headboard, when he rolled me over onto the bed. On my knees—he liked me that way, and I liked it even more—his cock parting my wet lips and driving in deep.

"Oh! God!" I clutched the pillow, burying my red face there, stifling my moans of almost-too-good-to-bear pleasure as he moved his hips in circles the way he knew I loved. "Harder! Oh, harder! Please!"

He obliged with a deep grunt and shift of his weight, the slapping sound of our sex filling the room as he pounded me into the bed. He was fully on me now, both of us working toward the same end, and he buried his face in my hair, his arms going under mine, pinning me, making me completely his.

"Ahhhhh Zoe, baby, it's so close," he whispered, sounding as if he wanted to wait, to hold off, and I arched and squeezed him, convincing him otherwise.

"Make me come," I gasped, turning my face, his mouth against my cheek now. "Please, please, ohhh please…"

He kissed my cheek, my closed eyelid, any place his mouth could reach, whispering, "I love you, I love you, oh baby, I love youuuuuu…"

I didn't say it back, but I felt it as he gave one last, hard thrust and shuddering sigh before beginning to fill me with his seed. I took all of it and my body asked for more, the delicious pulsing of my pussy trying to squeeze every last bit of his cum. When he rolled to the side, slipping an arm across my back, I sighed, lamenting the loss of his weight.

"There she is, right on cue." Ian chuckled as Rachel called from the other room. She couldn't talk yet, but she made sounds, and this one meant "Come get me!" in no uncertain terms.

I smiled as he slipped out of bed, pulled on a pair of shorts, and headed toward the door. He didn't hesitate to love her, just like he'd been with me.

"Ian."

He stopped, turning to look at me, still naked and sex-flushed on the bed. His eyes were hungry, and I knew mine were too. "God, you're beautiful," he breathed, almost as if he were saying it to someone else, as if I weren't even there.

"Ian, I'm going to have a baby."

His startled eyes met mine, his face a stunned mask for a moment, and then a smile broke through, broke my heart into a million pieces, shattered it forever and left it unusable for anyone else but him.

"Are you sure?"

I nodded. "Pretty sure."

He ran a hand through his dark hair, blinked a few times, and then laughed. "I can't believe it."

I smiled, stretched, rolled over and pulled up the sheet, basking in the glow of his delight. In the other room, Rachel started to cry in earnest, used to being responded to by now.

"Guess I better take care of the first one before I contemplate the next one." He grinned, opening the door, and we both heard Jack pounding up the stairs.

"People!" Jack stopped in the doorway looking tired, sounding out of breath. "There's a whole group of them, coming this way."

People. Human beings had a way of bringing along strange things with them in this new world. The stranger in the woods had stolen my innocence and left me with a love greater than I could have imagined in the form of my daughter. Then Jack and I had been alone again, and we hadn't seen another human being since Ian and Susan had arrived at our doorstep—and that had, again, brought me one of the greatest joys of my life. My eyes met Ian's and I wondered what this new group of people might bring?

* * * *

There were six of them crowded around our little table. Jack had brought in folding chairs from the garage that we hadn't used in years, and they all ate my soup and said how grateful they were for it. The big guy, Josh, the one who seemed to be the leader, peppered us with questions about how we lived, how we still had some power, fresh water, vegetables and fruits. I told him what I knew about what Papa had done, how he had made our home sustainable long before the collapse.

"It doesn't matter, Josh," the one called Stephen insisted. "They've got all this and more up north!"

And Ian, of course, wanted to know. I sat on the kitchen floor, serving as a human gate for Rachel from the crowded kitchen table, and let her pull out all of Mama's pots and pans and bang them. I sat and watched, listening to the talk of electric power, running water, cars, computers, and a brand new government. Jack watched and listened, too. I saw his eyes moving from face to face as the conversation moved, grew heated, insistent.

"You need to come with us!" Josh squeezed Ian's shoulder. "They need smart guys like you and me up there. The world is coming back—civilization! What a concept!"

What a concept. I contemplated it as Rachel gleefully found another game to play, pulling herself up to standing using the open cupboard door. The things I might have once wanted for my child—a good education, a college fund, gainful employment, a big, lovely wedding and grandchildren to spoil—no longer seemed to matter. They didn't matter for me anymore, and they certainly didn't matter for her.

What did I want for my baby? *Babies.* I covered my belly protectively with my hand as I listened to them talk, debate, argue. I watched Ian, wondering what he was thinking. Did he agree with them, that it was all inevitable, the resurrection of government, civilization? What had been so civilized about it, anyway? They were talking about people who liked to be in charge—those were the people who had taken away my parents, my whole life as I'd known it. It had been their short-sightedness that had left Jack and I orphaned and alone.

But I wasn't alone anymore. Rachel took her first step toward me with an excited squeal, throwing her chubby arms around my neck, and I laughed, hugging her close, shutting out the sound of other voices. My whole world was here in my arms, here in this house, and I didn't want to leave it. When I opened my eyes, I saw Ian looking at me, not smiling, just watching, his eyes questioning.

"I have to put the baby to bed," I murmured, working my way past the strangers in my kitchen and toward the bedroom. I couldn't bear to hear any more and wanted a safe place to hide.

* * * *

I knew, somehow, it was going to be an argument. I knew he was going to want to go with them—it was where he'd been heading before he found his way here to me. Of course he wanted to go.

"Think of it, Zoe," Ian whispered in the dark. I hated whispering in my own house, knowing there were people sleeping on my couch and my floor. "Think of everything we'll be able to give Rachel—and our new baby." His hand moved over my belly and I cringed. I never would have thought I could possibly have such a reaction, and yet there it was.

"I can't." The words were choked, and it was all I could manage. He'd been talking for so long, dreaming about the future, an impossible future I couldn't even begin to imagine, and I knew my words would stop him cold. And they did.

"Zoe, don't say that." He buried his face in my hair.
"Of course you're coming."

I shook my head. "No. I can't."

Beside me, he stiffened, moving slightly away. "Can't...or won't?"

I shrugged. "Does it matter?"

I hid my face when he turned on the light so he could pack. I hid my feelings, too, refusing to cry even when he sat on the bed and touched my shoulder, shaking me gently.

"Zoe, I want you with me."

My voice was muffled. "If you wanted me, you'd stay."

"Damnit, I love you." He sounded desperate and in pain. But so was I.

"So prove it."

He snorted. "I'm supposed to go backwards in time, when we have an opportunity for a real life, to prove I love you?"

"Is that what it's been like here for you? Are we so backwards? Hasn't this been real enough for you?" The tears trembled, on the verge, but I refused to let them fall.

"That's not what I meant."

"Actions speak louder than words." I turned away from him. "If you want to go, then go."

"I want to go," he agreed, stroking my hair. "And I want you to go with me."

"I can't."

When he left, I cried myself to sleep.

* * * *

"Where's Ian?"

Startled, I woke up to find Jack sitting on my bed. The sun was just coming up and I blinked at him in the faint light. I felt the weight of Ian's absence the moment conscious thought entered my mind.

"He's going with them," I whispered hoarsely.

"Are you?"

I shook my head. "I don't want to go."

"Me neither," Jack agreed.

"What are we going to do?" I reached for his hand, squeezing it.

"I have an idea." He stood, his eyes hardening. "I want to show you something. Get dressed...and bring the baby."

There was no sense arguing with Jack. Like a robot, I dressed, both myself and a half-asleep Rachel who blinked up at me in surprise at being the one woken instead of the other way around. I found Jack in the kitchen waiting for me, a bag slung over his shoulder. Low snores came from the living room and I knew our guests were still asleep. Glancing in, I saw Ian asleep among them, his head resting on the bag he'd packed the night before. The sight of him filled me with so much emotion I had to turn away to choke it down.

"Come on," Jack urged.

I followed, letting him lead me blindly through a path in the woods. It wasn't a familiar one to me, but we had acres upon acres of land back here and it would take decades to explore it all. The sun was coming up for real now, not playing peek-a-boo with the horizon anymore, and I shaded my eyes against its light as we came to a clearing.

"Oh my god! Jack, did you—?"

The question fell away from my lips, because of course he did. Who else? The little honeycomb he'd fashioned in the cellar laboratory was nothing compared to this one. It was as tall at the trees that grew up back here, and almost as wide.

"I never could figure out why the bees would want to come back," Jack mused as he took a step toward the enormous thing he'd built. Each hexagon was easily big enough for a human to walk through. "Somehow they managed to build the perfect structure, something that would send them...I don't know. Back in time? Into another dimension? A better world?"

He shook his head, as if he were trying to work it out. Rachel clamored to get down and I set her on the grass, walking to where Jack was standing so I could touch the thing. It was smooth, waxy...truly beautiful and amazing.

"But then I realized, all of the things they bring us...Zoe, they were bringing it back to us. They went away and came back with things to heal us. They made their healing honey, and pollinated our food. That was their purpose." He turned to me, grasping my hands. "And now, I'm wondering...what if it's our turn?"

"What do you mean?"

His eyes searched mine, as if he could find an answer there. "Maybe I figured this out for a reason. Maybe the humans are supposed to go there and bring something back...so we can heal this place, this planet."

I blinked at him in surprise.

"Zoe, it's so beautiful over there, so perfect. Do you remember?"

I tried not to, but of course I did. The air was clean, so clean it hurt. Everything seemed brighter—more. We hadn't wanted to go far at first—I was too afraid of losing the place where we'd come in, that we might not find it again—but like Hansel and Gretel, we left a trail of torn scraps of Jack's shirt tied onto tree limbs and went exploring. Our woods were nothing compared to this place, as if we'd finally found the land of milk and honey, a true garden of Eden.

"I want to go," Jack said, and his words made my heart lurch, remembering Ian's plea the night before. "Please come with me."

I thought of staying here, how people would just keep coming. Eventually, they would rebuild, and nothing would be any different than it had been before. I didn't know if Jack's theory was right or not—but I did know I wouldn't run into anyone who talked about computers and cars and government on the other side of the honeycomb. And whatever infected the bees when they were here would infect us again, too. It was inevitable.

"Rachel!"

I gasped in surprise at Ian's voice. He strode through the clearing, still carrying his bag, pointing and yelling, but I couldn't comprehend it—all that would register was that it was Ian, my Ian, he'd followed us. He was here, not gone.

"Zoe! Get Rachel!"

I turned toward the honeycomb and saw her crawling into one of the holes. She wasn't walking well enough yet to toddle in and there wasn't anything to pull herself up on, but she had managed to crawl to the end of the hexagon, toward that strange pyramid-shaped point, the place I remembered seemed to soften and even *melt* as Jack as I slipped through.

I moved toward her, but it was too late. She was gone. One minute she was grinning her couple-toothed baby grin over her shoulder, and the next, she was through, disappeared, on the other side of the honeycomb. Ian broke into a run, crossing the distance easily, and I grabbed him before he could dive in after her.

"Ian!" I put myself between him and the giant honeycomb. "Jack and I are leaving."

He blinked at me, as if trying to make sense of my words.

"Rachel...Rachel's going, too. In fact..." I laughed, squatting down to peer into the hole. "Rachel went first."

Ian squatted down, too, staring at the place she'd been. "What are you talking about?"

"Do you trust me?" I asked, tears in my eyes as I looked at him.

He reached for my hand, nodding.

"Do you love me?"

"Zoe, I never would have left." He stood and pulled me close, and I knew it was all going to be okay. "I wouldn't have left you and Rachel and the baby...never. I couldn't."

"Then let's go."

I took his hand in one of mine, and Jack's in the other, and together we went through a gateway to a whole new world where my daughter was waiting for us, sitting in field of wildflowers and waiting for her life to begin.

Author's Note:

No one knows why the bees are disappearing, although speculation abounds—poor nutrition, viruses, pesticides, antibiotics, genetically modified crops, climate change, electromagnetic radiation—but everyone agrees that if they continue to die at the rate they are, the world's food supply could become seriously low. Currently, no one knows what causes autism either—although many of the above speculations have also been made about the disorder.

Core Deep

Twenty-six degrees below zero, almost total darkness and white-out conditions, but Mary didn't notice any of it as Finn trudged up behind her, the thick cloud of his breath misting over her shoulder as he watched her work.

"What's your depth?" He had to yell to be heard over both the drill and the generator running it, but Mary didn't acknowledge his question, too engrossed, determined. Another ten feet. And then another. She'd pulled two cores on her own already—they were bagged and tagged on the sled she'd dragged along behind her on the snowmobile to the site. Both her shoulders and her head ached, but she didn't care.

He moved to help her as the mechanical swirl of the drill began to rise to the top, like a dark barber's pole or a terrible, twisted candy cane. It was heavy without an ice core in its center, but twice that now with its frigid contents. Mary stepped aside, letting him lift it out of her hands, pulling it free and turning it sideways, carrying it over to the makeshift work station. She'd set that up, too, in only the glow from one generator-powered work light. It was December twenty-second, the eve of the winter solstice, and they had officially moved into twenty-four hour darkness at the North Pole.

"We're at almost four thousand meters." The steam of her breath joined his as they bent over the thick length of ice, together sweeping chips from its surface with small brushes. The tubular metal cradle it rested in measured the core down to the millimeter.

Finn sat back on his haunches and gave a low whistle. "Christ, Mare. That's deeper than anyone's ever gone. Ever. And this is firn."

The excitement in her belly burned almost as hot as her cheeks and she nodded, noting the measurement in a notebook she pulled from her pocket. The pens they had were the same ones astronauts used in space. Regular ink froze quickly out here. She'd finally grown used to handling pens and other small instruments with thick gloves on instead of the thin latex she was used to.

Glancing over at Finn, watching him work as he wrote out a label and pressed it onto the surface of the polyethylene bag, she thought that only he would be crazy enough to suggest running off to the North Pole in the dead of winter. But she'd been wrong. There were plenty of others on the team at first, with the goal of providing the deepest and most comprehensive Arctic ice core data ever collected in the hopes of helping boost the research on climate change. She had jumped at the chance to work with firn—snow so cold all the time it never melted from year to year—and, too, with Finn.

Without Finn, she never would have known about this opportunity, let alone taken it, leaping with a blind faith the girl her father had once called "Miss Microscope" would never have considered without the solidity of her best friend, Finn, beside her. As one of the world's most renowned paleoclimatologists, he'd been on hundreds of Arctic expeditions. She'd been naively excited beyond words when they started this project, at the thought of being a part of history, and too, of spending time away from the world with Finn. And now that the rest of the crew had left, going home just in time for the holidays and leaving them to finish up the last of their project, they were truly alone.

Mary rubbed her gloved finger over the surface of the core—ice frozen for seven-hundred and fifty thousand years and pulled from a depth of almost two and a half miles. No human being had ever touched anything so deep before. If the bitter cold didn't do it, the incredible rush of that realization should have been more than enough to give her goose bumps under her parka, but that wasn't what caused the shiver that ran up her spine, nor was it the heat from Finn's body next to hers.

She had discovered something even more bottomless, more infinite. And she was hungry for more, determined to prove to Finn that what she'd found wasn't some statistical anomaly.

"I'm going deeper." She stood, turning toward the drill, leaving him to bag and tag the latest core, but Finn caught her arm, shaking his head.

"It's enough." He nodded toward the sled. "Let's pack up and get back to base. It's freezing, it's midnight and you're sick."

"I'm not sick." Looking longingly at the drill, she sighed and let him lead her to the snowmobile. He sat her on the seat, pulling her parka hood around her face as if she were a child. "Finn! A ninety-nine degree fever doesn't qualify as sick!" She brushed his coat-tightening hands away. "Would you quit?"

"I'll pack us up." He gave her a long, steady look. "Okay?"

She relented, sitting back down to wait. It didn't take him long to break it all down and pack it onto the sled. Her head did ache, and her face burned, but she was sure it was more from the bone-numbing chill than from her little fever. It was just a cold, but he acted like she was at death's door. The thought of examining the cores she'd pulled that night perked her up as Finn climbed onto his snowmobile, starting it and motioning her to follow.

They had a thick dark rope running from their drill site to the base half a mile away so they wouldn't get stuck out in the snow in white-out conditions and could always find their way back. Their camp, now empty of the rest of the crew, consisted of an insulated trailer with a huge satellite dwarfing its dark surface mounted outside. That was where they slept and ate, but the lab was built mostly underground, and that's where they parked to unload.

"You stay here!" Finn cradled one of the cores in two hands, turning sideways to take it down into the lab.

She'd never met a man so good at giving orders. He would have made a great drill sergeant—if he wasn't such a brilliant scientist. Mary slid off the Arctic Cat, killing the engine before hefting a second core from the sled and heading down after him. He gave her a sour look as he passed, heading back out for the third one and the rest of the equipment. What was he going to do—fire her? It didn't matter out here in the middle of nowhere. She'd directly defied him and returned to the site to drill tonight, and she had no intention of following any more orders, except perhaps the insistent ones in her own head. It had always been her motivation—her curiosity, that sense of discovery. She had to know.

The lab had been built months before the crew arrived. It was a wonder of modern engineering, a simple, elegant self-supporting steel arch which could take the great load of snow without even one internal support. Their grant had paid for everything, even the heavy airlocked door that opened up to what was paradise compared to the work environment outside. Ambient air temperature remained at a constant seventeen degrees Fahrenheit underground, quite balmy compared to the negative temperatures above. Drifting snow—the kind they had now, white-out moving toward blizzard conditions—were only a factor because they had to maintain access to the portal.

She turned on the light and the arctic fluorescents, resistant to cold, flickered and came alive. To Mary, it was heaven, and she flipped her hood back, her lungs aching with the change in temperature, sucking air not quite as sharp and bitter as before. She'd never been so aware of her own body as she had become on this trip. The extremes of the environment had forced her to acknowledge her own corporeal nature, something the safety of a job in her lab at home back in Massachusetts had never compelled her to do. Sure, they had winter there, a change of seasons...but nothing like this, the deep, constant incomprehensible cold.

"Come on, Mare." Finn had the third core, kicking the door shut behind him. "Let's go to bed."

She looked up from where she was sliding the first core she'd drilled out of its bag. *He didn't mean together, dummy.* But her heart felt as if it were beating somewhere in her throat and she was glad her cheeks were still red from the cold to cover their flush. Instead of answering him, she finished sliding the bag free and set the core into the cradle of the scale, recording the weight in another section of her notebook.

"You are so stubborn." Finn watched as she traded her thick gloves for latex, inspecting the length of ice for a crack-free sample and, using a fine saw, separating it out.

"And you are so bossy," she countered, cutting off a few millimeters of the sample, weighing the largest section on another scale and recording the reading. Five-hundred-and-two grams. Perfect. Selecting a smaller polyethylene bag, she placed the sample inside and then set it into their flash cooler. It would take the sample down to negative eighty degrees Celsius.

"You're really going to do this tonight?" He sighed as she began sawing at another length of the core. This one she would put into the plasma mass spectrometer.

"Go to bed, Finn." She waved him away as she inspected the sample, her trained eyes looking for cracks or imperfections.

He pulled his own heavy gloves off and reached for a sterile latex pair. "I'm not going without you."

She smiled, holding up her sample like a trophy. "Then fire up Old Bessie, because I need to see this reading or I'm never going to be able to sleep."

They worked well together—they always had—their timing in sync, anticipating one another's next motion with a deft precision that came from years of moving together in the same space. Finn took the sample from her hand and carried it over to "Old Bessie"—their plasma mass spectrometer. Compact and light, it was the size of a small television and attached to a laptop for reading output.

Mary used an instrument they jokingly called "the tweezers" to extract the frigid sample from the freezing unit and lift it carefully out of the bag. It was a perfect record of history, an effective time capsule, storing a snapshot of the earth's atmosphere seven-hundred-and-fifty thousand years ago. The tests would tell them the age of the ice within a few years here or there. It would also tell them all the common meteorological data from that time period—precipitation amount, solar activity, air temperature, atmospheric composition.

But she wasn't interested in any of that. The millions of tiny air bubbles in the ice had revealed something to her even more amazing than greenhouse gases or evidence of climate change.

"Into the cheese grater with you." Mary placed the sample into a round, stainless steel extraction flask, closing the door and turning on the machine. It would grind the ice into fine chips in a vacuum, release the air and trap the gasses without any contamination to taint the sample. This, too, was attached to a laptop, and the results would be analyzed by computer.

She couldn't resist coming to watch for the results of the spectrometer over Finn's shoulder. The laptop just showed a slow-moving bar that read, "Analyzing - Please Wait" beneath. His hood was thrown back, and she noted the way his jaw clenched and unclenched, the way he pointedly didn't turn to look over his shoulder at her.

She also noticed the way his dark hair curled at the nape of his neck—long, too long. He needed a cut, but of course there was nowhere to get one out there. She wondered if he would let her do it, and just imagining running her fingers through the black raven's wings of his hair made her feel breathless.

"Well, there it is." Finn sounded annoyed as he pointed to the screen and she almost laughed.

"I told you the last one wasn't a contaminated sample." She fought the smug urge to stick her tongue out at his back.

He rolled his eyes, pulling his latex gloves off and reaching for his warmer ones. "Two samples don't make it conclusive."

"Did you run it through the gas chromatograph?"

"Does Old Bessie moo?"

Mary touched the laptop screen, pointing to one of the longer spikes. "So this one here..."

"Unidentifiable."

"Finn! Look!" She grabbed a three-ring-binder from the table, flipping it open and holding it up next to the screen. "It's exactly the same as the last one. Look at the graph."

"I'm looking." He was looking, but he wasn't happy about it.

"And this..." She turned the other laptop on the counter, which had already finished analyzing its own data, so he could see the reading from the other machine. "See here? It's the same. Unidentified."

Finn shrugged. "It doesn't necessarily mean anything."

"What are you afraid of?" She couldn't believe his nonchalance, his lack of curiosity about this new discovery.

He quickly turned off the power to the laptop, not even shutting it down the way he should have. "I'm afraid you're feverish and I'm going to have to radio us out of here before you start hallucinating."

Hurt, she felt her chest tightening and she confronted him with her hands on her hips. "I'm not hallucinating lab results, Finn."

"Okay, so you got the results you were looking for," he snapped, reaching over and stabbing the power button on the other laptop. "Can we go to bed now?"

Her face and body felt frozen, colder than she'd ever been out in the arctic chill. "I bet you every single one of these deeper cores will show us the same thing. It's getting stronger, you know, more concentrated, the deeper we go."

He shrugged again, turning toward the door, a dismissal.

"There's something down there!" She wanted to throw something at his head and her hands clenched into fists. "Something no one has ever discovered before!"

"Well, if it's down there, it will still be there in the morning, won't it?" he asked over his shoulder, opening the door and letting in a blast of frigid air. "Are you coming?"

She'd butted heads with him before—they'd had playful, week-long disagreements back and forth sometimes. But she had never experienced him like this—cold, dismissive, obdurate.

Her righteous elation dampened by his reaction, Mary snapped her own gloves off and reached for her warm ones, the action an assent, and he watched her put them on before he went out the door. She knew he expected her to follow him, and she did, feeling dizzy with her discovery and his trivialization of it. Leaving everything, she just turned out the light and shut the door behind her.

Her cheeks felt as if they were on fire as she trudged after him in the powder, and the cold hit her like a wall, actually stopping her breathless in the dark. Finn's retreating back, heading toward the trailer, was just visible through the blowing snow. Her heart hammered hard in her chest, her legs like lead, and she managed to call out to him once before she went down to her knees.

"Finn!"

For a minute she thought he wasn't going to stop, that he was going to childishly storm off and leave her. And she didn't think she could get back up. Her legs felt too weak, trembling, and she let her body go, collapsing on the snow and rolling to her back, giving up. It didn't matter. He didn't believe her, he didn't care. None of it mattered. The stars were bright jewels in a velvet sky, so close she felt she could reach out and touch them, and she actually stretched a hand out into the darkness.

Then he was kneeling over her, wedging his arms beneath, lifting.

"I think I'm sick," she murmured.

"Ya think?" His gruff comment was the last thing she remembered before the stars blinked out.

* * * *

She woke up shivering in a cold sweat to find him beside her. She sensed more than saw him—it was completely dark, their rooms were small, his knees pressed right up against the edge of her cot as he shifted in the chair.

"Finn?"

"I'm here." His voice was soft, and there was no anger in it.

She rolled toward him, clutching his knee, sure now. She didn't know if it had been the fever that had given her the sudden flash of realization, or if it was just something that had bubbled up from below her consciousness, a deeper intuition. "I know what it is."

His answer couldn't have surprised her more. "So do I." His hand pressed against her forehead but she was cool now, almost clammy, and he stated the obvious.

"Your fever broke."

"No, I mean...what we found." She swallowed, sitting up cross-legged, her back against the wall, her bare knees pressed to his denim-clad ones. He'd undressed her down to her flannel shirt before putting her to bed, and the thought might have embarrassed her if she hadn't been so eager to tell him what she knew. "I know what it is!"

"So do I," he said again, reaching for the light on the small table, turning it on. She was too aware now of her state of undress, the way her dark, tousled hair fell around her face. She ran a hand through its length, smoothing, looking at him watching her, his face unreadable, his gaze moving quickly up from the "v" of her flannel to meet her eyes. He picked up a stoppered test tube off the table and held it up. "I've been in the lab for hours tonight, testing samples."

"What time is it?" she croaked.

"Near morning, I guess." He shrugged. Morning didn't mean much out here without the sun. They were living blind, groping around for answers in the darkness, and the metaphor didn't escape her as Finn offered her the test tube. "This is what you found."

She took it, peering in at the crystallized substance in the bottom. "It's a solid?"

"Yeah." He snorted. "And a gas. And a liquid. I've run every test we have, and the computer's analyzed the data in every possible configuration imaginable, and it all comes up the same."

"Unidentifiable," she murmured, staring at it, amazed. "And atomic structure? This...it's got to be a new element."

Her breathless wonder was broken by Finn revealing another piece of even more unlikely information. "It has no atomic weight, Mare."

"That's not possible." She just stared at him.

"I know." He shook his head, half-smiling, and shrugged. "It has volume, it has mass, it takes up space. But you can't measure it. *It has no atomic weight.*"

"But..."

Just when she was coming to terms with that impossible fact, he dropped another, equally as implausible, into her lap. "It also has no half-life."

"What?" She held the sample up to the light, frowning. "Are you sure you tested it right? Maybe there's something wrong with the computer..."

"Please." Rolling his eyes, he sat back in the chair with a sigh. "I've been calculating atomic weight and half-life since I was in high school. Everything decomposes and gives off some sort of radiation, right? *But this doesn't.* The graph won't move—it's a solid flatline. This stuff is...it's infinite. It's some sort of infinite energy source..."

"I know." Mary couldn't begin to explain her feeling, the certainty of her strangely drawn conclusion. She had no logical basis for it, although Finn's research was going a long way toward convincing the Miss Microscope part of her that her intuition was correct. Taking a deep breath, she closed her eyes, and just said it, "It's God."

When Finn didn't respond—she'd expected laughter, at the very at least, coupled with a sarcastic comment—she opened her eyes to look at him. He was thoughtful, staring at the test tube in her closed fist. She went on, "You feel it just as much as I do. I know you do. What we've discovered...all the laws and rules of physics, of the entire universe, just turned upside down. This proves—"

"This doesn't prove anything." He did laugh then, shaking his head. "You might as well say we just proved the existence of Santa Claus. It would hold about as much weight in the scientific community. Hell, why not? We're at the North Pole, aren't we? Let's just call the new element Santa Clausium!"

"I think..." She took a deep breath, ignoring his sarcasm, and pushed forward. "I think it's here for a reason."

"Well, in that sense, I guess everything's here for a reason."

"No, I mean here." She waved her hand around. "Up here. In the Arctic. Frozen at that particular depth."

"What do you mean?" He frowned.

"I think it wanted to be frozen."

It took a moment for him to respond. "Are you saying...this substance... is *sentient?*"

She ignored his disbelief. "I also think it wanted to be found."

He laughed. "I think maybe your fever's back."

"It's everything and nothing all at once." She reached out, opened his fist, and put the test tube in it. He looked down at their hands, and then back at her, his eyes searching. "It's an *infinite source*. What else, Finn? What else could it be?"

He opened his mouth to deny it, she knew him well enough to know, but she pressed her fingertips to his lips, shaking her head. "Don't think. Just feel. Hold it in your hand and feel it."

It was an incredibly unscientific request, but he swallowed and did as she asked. Shaking his head, looking pained, she knew he was struggling with the part of him that required facts, proof. He had them now in his very hand, and still his mind wanted to deny it. She searched his face as he opened his eyes and knew which part of him had won.

"It's everything. It's nothing." His voice actually trembled and she nodded, silently agreeing. "It's limitless power. For good or evil, that's what this means."

The idea was thrilling, beyond words, and she naively mused aloud for a moment. "In the right hands..."

Finn shook his head, his eyes flashing. "In the *wrong* ones..."

The endless possibility of that thought hung there between them. Mary closed her eyes with the weight of it, leaning her head back against the wall. She felt like crying, laughing, screaming. It was in her, everything at once, almost too much to bear.

"Are you okay?" His hand was warm on her forehead and she wanted to turn her face to it, encourage him to touch her, to bridge the gap. "Fever?"

"No." She opened her eyes, watching his hand fall to his lap. "Just...it's..." She shrugged, unable to say, but he nodded.

"I know."

This time it was her voice that trembled when she asked, "What are we going to do?"

Finn closed his eyes again, pursed his lips, that pained look briefly crossing his face for a moment before he looked at her and said, "The right thing."

The right thing.

Mary reached for the test tube, meaning to take it from him, set it aside, but he caught her hand, turning it over. She thought he was going to place the substance there, but instead he lifted her palm and kissed it, his breath hot against the sensitive inside of her wrist, his lips impossibly soft.

She stared at him in wonder, daring to ask, "So, just what is the right thing, Finn?"

"Right now?" His eyes searched hers, looking for an answer that had always been there. "Right now, it's this."

There was no resistance in her. She let him lean in and capture her mouth, press her back and then down onto the cot, welcoming the weight of him. She heard the faint "tink" of the test tube hitting the floor and then rolling as they came together on the small confines of her little bed, mouths slanting, tongues seeking heat.

Never had she wanted him more. If she could have cracked herself open to the core, absorbed him completed into her, she would have. Instead, she wound herself around him by degrees, her fingers in his hair, her legs twined with his, her arms snaking around his neck, her tongue circling the hot recesses of his mouth. Finn didn't object. His hands roamed up under her flannel, exploring the soft valley of her waist, the indent of her navel, and— oh, god, finally—the sloping curve of her breast, the rise of her hardening nipple.

Her room was never warm. She went to bed every night nearly fully dressed, but now she was suddenly hot, more than feverish, her body on fire with a heat that could melt ice. Eager, she tugged his dark turtleneck out from the waistband of his jeans, her hands roaming the hard arch of his back, the wings of his shoulder blades, his muscles tight and thick but melting under her touch. Finn helped her pull his shirt off, and she took a brief, breathless moment to admire the broad, masculine emerging shadow of him above her before her trembling fingers found the buttons on her own shirt, working her way down while he worked up from the bottom. Their hands met in the middle.

He looked at her and groaned when she revealed herself, shrugging out of the shirt, wearing nothing then but the thin barrier of her panties rubbing against the hard press of denim between her thighs. He caught one of her dark-tipped nipples between his lips, his tongue bathing it with the heat of his mouth, a shocking juxtaposition to the cool air. Her body arched all on its own, her hand moving between them, seeking the softness of her mound and the hard press of his cock as they rocked together.

Finn gasped when she cupped her hand over the denim bulge and then pressed his hips forward hard, trapping her hand, his mouth covering hers, tongue plunging deep. His excitement made her bold and she quickly unbuttoned and unzipped him, maneuvering to slide her hand in and pull the length of him out.

"Oh god," he murmured against her throat, nuzzling there, making her nipples stand up as she stroked him against the inside of her thigh.

Yes, God, she thought, feeling it, something, coursing through her as they moved closer toward coupling, her mind flashing momentarily on the impossible, unknown crystallized substance resting in a test tube underneath them somewhere. She wanted to tell Finn how incredible it was, how perfectly divine, but when she looked into his eyes, she thought he already knew.

"Off," she insisted, shoving his jeans and boxers down his hips. He obliged, both of them naked now except for the brush of her panties, which were gone in a whisper as he reached down there to touch her.

She wanted him inside of her, now, forever—she couldn't wait. He was as hard as bedrock in her hand, and she rubbed the tip of him up and down her slit, displacing his probing fingers and making him shudder in response, his hips already moving.

"Please," he begged, looking down at her with half-closed eyes. "Oh, god, Mary, I need you..."

"Yes."

She opened to him completely then, and he took her, his cock aimed to perfection, drilling deep, making her gasp with his precision. She didn't let him go, grinding her hips upward, wrapping her legs around his, seeing him grit his teeth, that pained look crossing his face for a moment, and she knew he was holding back.

"No," she whispered, rolling her hips, meeting his beginning thrusts. "Don't hold back, Finn. Please. I want you. All of you."

He took a quivering breath, shaking his head, his eyes wild, hungry. "If you knew..."

"I do know." She touched his cheek, traced his lips, feeling the pulse of him buried in the hot recesses of her body, every muscle taut, waiting for him to let go. It was beyond pleasure, beyond sensation itself, just out of reach, as if waiting for them to catch up. "I feel it. Don't you feel it?"

"Yes." The look of bewildered longing in his eyes made her slip her hand behind his head, pulling his mouth to hers and kissing him hard as he began to move in her. They rocked together, the heat of their bodies, their breath, filling the little room.

There was no holding back now, their soft cries melting together as they moved toward some blissful destination shimmering on the horizon, and she watched it recede with every motion forward, an aching mirage. Desperate, greedy, she clung to him as if he could take her there, the thick pound of his cock driving her hard against the cot as she begged him for more.

"Harder," she gasped into his ear, her teeth raking his neck, his shoulder. "Oh Finn, please, I'm..."

"Coming," he groaned, thrusting deep and she felt it burst, the energy trapped between them released in a bright, white hot explosion.

"There," she whispered, her eyes closing, her body giving in to the sensation, expanding, contracting, filled with everything and nothing all at once. Eternity had never been so close.

There wasn't room for them both on the little cot, but Finn made himself her bed, rolling beneath her, finding the edge of her sleeping bag and pulling it over them for warmth. There weren't words, and Mary didn't miss them. Instead, she pressed her cheek against his chest, listening to the steady beat of his heart, and felt nothing but awe as they drifted off together toward some even deeper destination.

* * * *

"You said we were going to do the right thing."

"This *is* the right thing, Mare." Finn was heading out the door, and she followed, like she always did, feeling small. "We're scientists. We can't possibly let this discovery go unreported. This is bigger than relativity!"

"And we know how well that turned out," she grumbled, pulling her parka hood closer as they headed toward the snowmobiles. He had loaded the ice cores she'd pulled onto the sled, and now meant to take them to the drop-off point. The helicopter he'd radioed would be there in less than an hour.

"We need bigger equipment to test this with," he insisted, reaching back and grabbing her hand, pulling her with him. "An accelerator, for one. We have to be sure we've found what we think we've found."

Mary stopped, pulling him up short, and he turned to look at her. "You're not sure?"

"I don't know." Finn shrugged. "That's what I want, though. I want to be sure."

"I'm sure."

"Good for you." He looked defiant, and it reminded her of the Finn she'd experienced the night before, in the lab.

"I know what we found." She caught both of his gloved hands in hers, squeezing so he could feel her. "I know what I felt. I know what I *feel.*"

"What does that have to do with anything?" He frowned, but his eyes softened when he looked at her face.

"It has everything to do with everything." She smiled, wanting to kiss the frown line creasing his forehead. "Finn, I love you. I've loved you for as long as I can remember."

"Aw, Mare..." He swallowed, looking away, down at the snow.

She took a deep breath. "Don't do this."

"I have to." His jaw tightened and he left her standing there, trudging toward the snowmobile. It was running, the headlight a beacon in the darkness. She turned, making her decision, knowing she couldn't go with him and turn their discovery over to the rest of the world.

"Hey!" His voice made her turn back. "Mary! Quick!"

She couldn't see well enough in the darkness, but his voice was panicked, and she broke into a run. The snow under her feet was lightly packed, but it had stopped falling at least, giving her a clear path to him.

"What's the matter?" she gasped, and then turned to where he was pointing, his eyes dark with anger.

"Did you do that?" His voice was angry, and she winced.

The bags on the back of the sled were empty. She knelt beside them, running her gloved hands over the surface. The ice cores were gone. They hadn't melted—there was no water or residue inside—and they hadn't evaporated, either, because the bags were completely flat, as if nothing had ever been in them in the first place.

Mary looked up and met Finn's accusing eyes. "I didn't. Finn, I've been with you the whole time!" It was true, and he knew it.

His shoulders slumped, his face falling. "Then what...how in the hell?"

She took his offered hand, letting him help her up. "I don't think we're supposed to understand."

"Oh fuck that." He threw up his hands, reaching over and turning off the snowmobile. "What the hell are we here for, if not to understand?"

"We can't see it...touch it...taste it..." She turned her face up to the sky, completely clear now, the stars even brighter than before. "We can just feel it."

"I don't feel anything," Finn growled, kicking at the sled.

"I think you do." She reached out and squeezed his gloved hand, feeling him give, just a little.

"Fuck," he muttered, but he slipped his arm around her waist, pulling her in closer.

"Look." She pointing to the horizon where a slow, lazy rainbow of colors danced in the sky—the aurora borealis, a rare event this time of year.

"Goddamnit, Mary." Finn's voice was choked as he pressed his lips to her forehead. "I love you. You know I do."

She smiled, her eyes filled with the ever-changing, infinite light of the universe, and spoke the truth with a certainty she'd never understood until that moment.

"I know."

Author's Note:

I wish what we were finding in ice cores really was an infinite source of energy. The world could certainly use one. According to a 2009 article in Science Daily (sciencedaily.com), ice cores are trying to tell us something, although not everyone is in agreement about what. Is global warming real? Will the polar ice caps do indeed melt further? The debate rages on, but the fact remains that 90% of the world's ice volume is in the Antarctic and the disappearance of even the smallest ice sheet could raise sea levels around the world by a staggering twenty feet.

Source: Science Daily (www.sciencedaily.com)

ABOUT SELENA KITT

Selena Kitt is a NEW YORK TIMES bestselling and award-winning author of erotic and romance fiction. She is one of the highest selling erotic writers in the business with over two million books sold!

Her writing embodies everything from the spicy to the scandalous, but watch out-this kitty also has sharp claws and her stories often include intriguing edges and twists that take readers to new, thought-provoking depths.

When she's not pawing away at her keyboard, Selena runs an innovative publishing company (excessica.com) and bookstore (excitica.com), as well as two erotica and erotic romance promotion companies (excitesteam.com and excitespice.com) and she now runs the Erotica Readers and Writers Association.

Her books EcoErotica (2009), The Real Mother Goose (2010) and Heidi and the Kaiser (2011) were all Epic Award Finalists. Her only gay male romance, Second Chance, won the Epic Award in Erotica in 2011. Her story, Connections, was one of the runners-up for the 2006 Rauxa Prize, given annually to an erotic short story of "exceptional literary quality."

Her book, Babysitting the Baumgartners, is now an adult film by Adam & Eve, starring Mick Blue, Anikka Albrite, Sara Luvv and A.J. Applegate.

She can be reached on her website at:
www.selenakitt.com

Did You Know?

BABYSITTING THE BAUMGARTNERS
Is Now a Motion Picture from Adam & Eve?

Starring
Anikka Albrite
Mick Blue
Sara Luvv
A.J. Applegate

Directed by Kay Brandt

BABYSITTING THE BAUMGARTNERS
By Selena Kitt

Ronnie—or as Mrs. Baumgartner insists on calling her, Veronica—has been babysitting for the Baumgartners since she was fifteen years old and has practically become another member of the family.

Now a college freshman, Ronnie jumps at the chance to work on her tan in the Florida Keys with "Doc" and "Mrs. B" under the pretense of babysitting the kids.

Ronnie isn't the only one with ulterior motives, though, and she discovers that the Baumgartners have wayward plans for their young babysitter.

This wicked hot sun and sand coming of age story will seduce you as quickly as the Baumgartners seduce innocent Ronnie and leave everyone yearning for more!

EXCERPT from
BABYSITTING THE BAUMGARTNERS:

When my legs felt steady enough to hold me, I got out of the shower and dried off, wrapping myself in one of the big white bath sheets. My room was across the hall from the bathroom, and the Baumgartner's was the next room over. The kids' rooms were at the other end of the hallway.

As I made my way across the hall, I heard Mrs. B's voice from behind their door. "You want that tight little nineteen-year-old pussy, Doc?"

I stopped, my heart leaping, my breath caught. *Oh my God.* Were they talking about me? He said something, but it was low, and I couldn't quite make it out. Then she said, "Just wait until I wax it for you. It'll be soft and smooth as a baby."

Shocked, I reached down between my legs, cupping my pussy as if to protect it, standing there transfixed, listening. I stepped closer to their door, seeing it wasn't completely closed, still trying to hear what they were saying. There wasn't any noise, now.

"Oh God!" I heard him groan. "Suck it harder."

My eyes wide, I felt the pulse returning between my thighs, a slow, steady heat. Was she sucking his cock? I remembered what it looked like in his hand--even from a distance, I could tell it was big--much bigger than any of the boys I'd ever been with.

"Ahhhh fuck, Carrie!" He moaned. I bit my lip, hearing Mrs. B's first name felt so wrong, somehow.

"Take it all, baby!"

All?! My jaw dropped as I tried to imagine, pressing my hand over my throbbing mound. Mrs. B said something, but I couldn't hear it, and as I leaned toward the door, I bumped it with the towel wrapped around my hair. My hand went to my mouth and I took an involuntary step back as the door edged open just a crack. I turned to go to my room, but I knew that they would hear the sound of my door.

"You want to fuck me, baby?" she purred. "God, I'm so wet ... did you see her sweet little tits?"

"Fuck, yeah," he murmured. "I wanted to come all over them."

Hearing his voice, I stepped back toward the door, peering through the crack. The bed was behind the door, at the opposite angle, but there was a large vanity table and mirror against the other wall, and I could see them reflected in it. Mrs. B was completely naked, kneeling over him. I saw her face, her breasts swinging as she took him into her mouth. His cock stood straight up in the air.

"She's got beautiful tits, doesn't she?" Mrs. B ran her tongue up and down the shaft.

"Yeah." His hand moved in her hair, pressing her down onto his cock. "I want to see her little pussy so bad. God, she's so beautiful."

"Do you want to see me eat it?" She moved up onto him, still stroking his cock. "Do you want to watch me lick that sweet, shaved cunt?"

I pressed a cool palm to my flushed cheek, but my other hand rubbed the towel between my legs as I watched. I'd never heard anyone say that word out loud and it both shocked and excited me.

"Oh God, yeah!" He grabbed her tits as they swayed over him. I saw her riding him, and knew he must be inside of her. "I want inside her tight little cunt."

I moved the towel aside and slipped my fingers between my lips.

He's talking about me!

The thought made my whole body tingle, and my pussy felt on fire. Already slick and wet from my orgasm in the shower, my fingers slid easily through my slit.

"I want to fuck her while she eats your pussy." He thrust up into her, his hands gripping her hips. Her breasts swayed as they rocked together. My eyes widened at the image he conjured, but Mrs. B moaned, moving faster on top of him.

"Yeah, baby!" She leaned over, her breasts dangling in his face. His hands went to them, his mouth sucking at her nipples, making her squeal and slam down against him even harder. "You want her on her hands and knees, her tight little ass in the air?"

He groaned, and I rubbed my clit even faster as he grabbed her and practically threw her off him onto the bed. She seemed to know what he wanted, because she got onto her hands and knees and he fucked her like that, from behind. The sound of them, flesh slapping against flesh, filled the room.

They were turned toward the mirror, but Mrs. B had her face buried in her arms, her ass lifted high in the air. Doc's eyes looked down between their legs, like he was watching himself slide in and out of her.

"Fuck!" Mrs. B's voice was muffled. "Oh fuck, Doc! Make me come!"

He grunted and drove into her harder. I watched her shudder and grab the covers in her fists. He didn't stop, though--his hands grabbed her hips and he worked himself into her over and over. I felt weak-kneed and full of heat, my fingers rubbing my aching clit in fast little circles. Mrs. B's orgasm had almost sent me right over the edge. I was very, very close.

"That tight nineteen-year-old cunt!" He shoved into her. "I want to taste her." He slammed into her again. "Fuck her." And again. "Make her come." And again. "Make her scream until she can't take anymore."

I leaned my forehead against the doorjamb for support, trying to control how fast my breath was coming, how fast my climax was coming, but I couldn't. I whimpered, watching him fuck her and knowing he was imagining me ... *me!*

"Come here." He pulled out and Mrs. B turned around like she knew what he wanted. "Swallow it."

He knelt up on the bed as she pumped and sucked at his cock. I saw the first spurt land against her cheek, a thick white strand of cum, and then she covered the head with her mouth and swallowed, making soft mewing noises in her throat. I came then, too, shuddering and shivering against the doorframe, biting my lip to keep from crying out.

When I opened my eyes and came to my senses, Mrs. B was still on her hands and knees, focused between his legs--but Doc was looking right at me, his dark eyes on mine.

He saw me. For the second time today--he saw me.

My hand flew to my mouth and I stumbled back, fumbling for the doorknob behind me I knew was there. I finally found it, slipping into my room and shutting the door behind me. I leaned against it, my heart pounding, my pussy dripping, and wondered what I was going to do now.

YOU'VE REACHED "THE END!"

BUY THIS AND MORE TITLES AT
www.eXcessica.com

Check us out for updates about eXcessica books!